"It was just a nightmare," she whispered to herself as she stepped to the window, hoping for a breath of air…. That's when she saw him.

He wore nothing but jeans and boots, a towel draped over one shoulder as he sauntered toward the pond.

He disappeared behind the trees. A moment later she heard a splash.

The sound pulled her—just as the thought of the cowboy in the cool water of the pond did.

She knew what could happen if she continued down to the pond. Just the thought sent a shiver through her. She took a step, then another. As she walked through the deep shadows of the trees, she felt excitement stir within her—and desire. She began to run.

At the edge of the trees, she stopped. She could see him swimming through the dark water, droplets washing over his brown skin, his back and shoulders shimmering in the moonlight.

She'd never seen a more beautiful man.

USA TODAY Bestselling Author

B.J. DANIELS

STAMPEDED

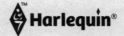

Harlequin®

TORONTO NEW YORK LONDON
AMSTERDAM PARIS SYDNEY HAMBURG
STOCKHOLM ATHENS TOKYO MILAN MADRID
PRAGUE WARSAW BUDAPEST AUCKLAND

This book is dedicated to Deb Lorene Mallory,
a fan and fellow writer who has become a good friend.
Thanks again for being such a wonderful guide that weekend in Billings. I had a great time and it was a treat to get to know you better.

Recycling programs
for this product may
not exist in your area.

ISBN-13: 978-0-373-74615-6

STAMPEDED

Copyright © 2011 by Barbara Heinlein

www.Harlequin.com

Printed in U.S.A.

ABOUT THE AUTHOR

USA TODAY bestselling author B.J. Daniels wrote her first book after a career as an award-winning newspaper journalist. That first book, *Odd Man Out,* received a four-and-a-half-star review from *RT Book Reviews* and went on to be nominated for Best Intrigue that year.

Daniels lives in Montana with her husband, Parker, and two springer spaniels, Spot and Jem. To contact her, write to B.J. Daniels, P.O. Box 1173, Malta, MT 59538 or email her at bjdaniels@mtintouch.net. Check out her website at www.bjdaniels.com.

Books by B.J. Daniels

CAST OF CHARACTERS

Marshall Chisholm—The cowboy didn't believe in a lot of things, including true love, until he met the beautiful psychic.

Alexa Cross—She'd spent her life keeping everyone at a distance to hide her secret. Could a house full of secrets and a neighboring cowboy change all that?

Landon Cross—He knew after he'd almost been killed in the old Wellington mansion that his sister Alexa was the only one who could save him.

Sierra Wellington Cross—It had been her idea to turn the old mansion into a bed-and-breakfast. But what else was she up to on those nights when her husband couldn't find her?

Archer and Carolina Durand and Gigi and Devlin Landers—The two young couples had offered to help Sierra and Landon remodel the old mansion. But was it out of boredom or was something else going on in that house?

Jayden Farrell—He was the odd man out, the only single friend who'd come along to help with the house. But was his interest in the house—or its owner, Sierra?

Tallulah Cross—The famous psychic might be dead, but she wasn't necessarily gone.

J. A. Wellington—Like the other Wellingtons, he'd left behind a deadly legacy along with the ghosts that haunted Wellington Manor.

Prologue

"Alexa? Alexa, wake up."

The five-year-old came awake with a start to find her mother beside her bed. Her heart thumped in her tiny chest.

"What is it, Mommy?" she asked, her voice breaking. Just the sight of her mother beside her bed in the middle of the night filled her with panic. She struggled to come out of her sleep. Had she been screaming in her sleep with another nightmare?

Sometimes when she had nightmares, she would wake up to find her mother beside her bed, standing motionless, staring down at her. Like now, her mother would have that strange, eerie look in her eyes, the one she got when she was working with her clients.

"Honey, I need you to sit up and do something for me."

Alexa loved her beautiful mother with her long, curly black hair, her wide violet eyes so like her own and the face of an angel. But she couldn't help the shiver that ran through her. Sometimes her mother scared her.

She rubbed sleep from her eyes and pushed herself up, blinking at the shaft of golden light that spilled across the floor from the hallway. Her mother always left the hall light on and the door cracked open a few inches because of Alexa's nightmares. The light from the hallway illuminated the empty, dark walls of her cavelike room.

"What were you thinking, Tallulah?" Alexa's father had demanded. "She's a child, a little *girl,* she should have a room painted pink with stuffed animals on the bed and clouds painted on the ceiling—not horrible black walls."

"The black walls will keep away the nightmares," her mother had argued.

But they hadn't. And her father had finally given up arguing and left before Alexa's baby brother had come along, and he'd never come back.

"It wasn't his spiritual path to be with us," her mother had told her when Alexa cried for her daddy. She missed the way he would hold her when she was frightened, the way he would smooth her long, wild dark hair with his big hand and the way he would rock her with soothing words until she fell back to sleep.

He used to call what Tallulah did for a living total nonsense. "Don't let it scare you, Alexa. It's all just mumbo jumbo, stuff your mother makes up for the fools who are silly enough to pay her."

"Alexa?" There was impatience in her mother's tone now.

She loved her mother and would do anything for her. The last thing she wanted was to disappoint her.

But she had seen how happy it made her mother when everyone commented on how much Alexa looked like her. Tallulah Cross wanted her daughter to be just like her in every way, and that was what frightened her more than the nightmares.

"Honey, I need you to look down at the end of your bed. What do you see?"

Her tiny stomach turned. She sensed how important this was to her mother. But Alexa didn't want to look. She wanted to close her eyes tight and make her mother and whatever might be at the end of the bed go away.

But she always did what her mommy asked

her. She was her mommy's good girl, her precious girl.

Alexa sat all the way up and took a breath, wrinkling her nose. The air smelled funny and she felt the way she did when she rubbed a balloon on her hair—her skin tingly, the space around her filled with static. Her body began to tremble under the covers as she slowly turned to look toward the end of her bed.

Tallulah Cross made her living in a small room at the front of their house. She told fortunes to the tourists who came through town by looking into the future and talking to those who'd gone to the other side. Dead people.

Alexa had overheard her mother telling her friends that her greatest hope in life was that, along with her beauty, she had passed her "gift" on to her daughter. For a long time, Alexa hadn't known what gift she was talking about.

Tonight, she knew. Just as she understood that this was a test and that if she wanted to be her mommy's "precious little girl," she must not disappoint her.

"What do you see, sweetie?" her mother asked, hope and something close to desperation in her voice.

Alexa tried not to flinch as she looked at the man standing at the end of her bed. He was tall. He stood funny, as if one leg was shorter than the other. But it was his face she would never forget, awake or asleep. Half of it was gone.

"You see the man, don't you, sweetie?"

A sob caught in her throat. "No, Mommy." It was the first lie she'd ever told and she instinctively knew it would come at a very high cost. But she didn't want to be just like her mother, even though it would mean she was no longer her mommy's special girl.

Alexa couldn't bear to see her mother's disappointment. Her heart ached as she closed her eyes, lay back down and pretended to go to sleep. It wasn't until she heard her mother leave the room that she opened them again and looked toward the end of her bed, knowing the man was still there. Nor had he been fooled.

He stared at her with that one dark eye, then he gave her a conspiratorial wink and vanished.

Alexa shut her eyes tight, fighting tears. She didn't want to see dead people. She didn't want them to talk to her. She told herself she wouldn't see them again. Nor would she see the future.

And she didn't for twenty-three years.

Chapter One

Marshall Chisholm was no carpenter. He was learning that the hard way, he thought. He put down his hammer for the day and turned to gaze out at the Montana landscape through what would one day be his finished bay window.

While he spent most of his days on the back of a horse herding cattle, he'd fallen in love with this house the moment he'd seen it. Not that there was anything special about it—or even the view. The house was a two-story farmhouse that had been built in the late 1930s. But it had good bones, as they say, and it had spoken to him the moment he'd walked in. Not that he would ever admit that.

There was something about the place that appealed to him even though it had been vacant for many years. He'd known it would take a lot of work, but he'd been eager to get started on it.

Along with the house, Marshall liked the view of the rolling prairie. It stretched out across this vast part of Montana as if endless. Out here, he felt on top of the world. Through every window he could see to the horizon with nothing to break that view on three sides but sagebrush and Black Angus cattle—his family's cattle.

The Chisholm Cattle Company ran more head of cattle than any other in the state and that took a lot of country. He also liked that as far as he could see, this was Chisholm land, most of it running to the horizon.

On the fourth side, the side this upstairs bedroom window faced, there were rolling grain fields and pasture, with only one structure on the horizon.

Marshall squinted as he noticed something different about the old three-story mansion in the distance. He'd looked at it many times since moving into this house. But this time he saw something odd.

Someone was over there.

That was such a rare occurrence that he picked up the binoculars he kept by the window and, peering through them, brought the huge mansion into focus.

He'd heard there had once been a small

settlement around the mansion called Wellington, but all the other buildings had been gone for years. The only structure that remained was the monster of a mansion, or Wellington Manor as the locals called it.

The massive, old place must have dwarfed the other buildings that had been there years before and would have been ostentatious even in these times, let alone a hundred years ago. He'd heard stories for years about the family and the house, though he'd never believed them. People liked to think that old places had ghosts.

The last resident of Wellington Manor had died a year ago, an old spinster niece of the original owner, Jedidiah Wellington. Marshall had heard the place was tied up in an estate.

He frowned as he noticed there was a small red sports car parked under the cottonwood trees that flanked the house. The cottonwoods were fed by a small spring-fed creek that ended in a pond at the end of the row of trees. Marshall liked to swim in the pond since it was halfway between his house and the mansion.

As he scanned the scene, he saw that there

was also a dark-colored large SUV parked behind the sports car.

How odd, he thought as he lowered the binoculars. Was it possible someone had bought the place? Or could it be squatters? His father had told him that drug dealers coming out of Canada would often stay in abandoned farmhouses, but he'd never seen anyone around Wellington Manor in the past year since it had been empty. The Canadian border was only about thirty miles away. The closest town to the south, Whitehorse, was another twenty miles. So the dirt road up to this part of the county didn't get a lot of traffic—let alone tourists. He supposed it could be drug runners.

Marshall took one more look through the binoculars and saw yet another vehicle coming up the long tree-lined drive to the mansion, this one a small white SUV.

He didn't know anyone who'd even been inside the mansion. Apparently Jedidiah Wellington and his family kept to themselves, and so had the old-maid niece who'd been the last one to live there.

His curiosity piqued and tired of carpentry work for the day, Marshall decided to saddle up and ride over to see what was going on.

ALEXA CROSS PULLED UP TO THE monstrous house with growing unease. The house looked like a hotel, looming three stories up with wings off four sides—not what she'd expected at all. When her brother had told her at the wedding that he and his new bride were remodeling her family's old house in Montana, she'd pictured something smaller, set in the mountains with lots of rock and wood. Not this ugly monstrosity.

As she stared at the house, she thought of his recent call saying he needed her to come out for a visit. She'd heard something in his voice that had scared her.

"What's wrong? Is it Sierra?"

"No," Landon had said, clearly irritated. "My wife's fine. *We're* fine."

Alexa wished now she'd never voiced her misgivings about her brother's hasty marriage. But she couldn't help worrying that he'd made a mistake and was now realizing it.

Both university students, Landon and Sierra had met while working in Yellowstone Park for the summer and had fallen in love. Alexa hadn't even gotten a chance to meet Sierra before the wedding held at the old hotel at Mammoth Hot Springs until the day before the ceremony.

Sierra Wellington wasn't the woman Alexa would have chosen for her brother, but she'd seen at once what had attracted Landon to the petite, pretty blonde. Landon, like Alexa, had taken after their mother. He had the curly, dark hair, the dark eyes and olive skin of what was rumored to be fortune-telling, gypsy ancestors.

The contrast between Landon and Sierra, Alexa was sure, had been part of their attraction for each other. That and a common denominator called Montana. Both had a tie to the state. Landon's father had allegedly been born here—at least that was what their mother had told them. Neither Alexa nor Landon had ever met the man. Nor had their mother apparently bothered to get the man's last name at the time of Landon's conception.

Sierra's roots ran deeper in Montana, with several generations of Montanans and a family house that still stood in what had been a town named after her great-great-grandfather.

"It's this house," her brother had said on the phone. "There's something wrong with it." When Landon had told her about the idea he and Sierra had to turn the mansion she'd inherited into a bed-and-breakfast, Alexa hadn't shared their enthusiasm.

"You mean structurally?" she'd asked, relieved it was nothing more earth-shattering than a construction problem. Neither her brother nor his wife knew anything about running a bed-and-breakfast, and Alexa questioned the feasibility when the closest town was Whitehorse—apparently a small western town with a declining population. Not to mention that this wide-open prairie part of Montana wasn't the one most tourists came to see.

She'd kept her reservations about their plan to herself though, fearing alienating her brother, who seemed as excited about the prospect as his wife.

"I know this is asking a lot, but I need you to come out here," Landon had said. "I want you to see the house and tell me what you think. What do you say, sis?"

What could she say? He was her only family, since their mother had died a year ago. She would do anything for him and he knew it. Also she felt honored that he wanted her opinion.

"I'll drive out this weekend." It was a

ten-hour drive from Spokane, Washington, where she lived and worked as a reporter. She could get a few days off from the newspaper without any trouble, and she hadn't seen her brother since the wedding and was worried about him.

"It might take more than a weekend," Landon had said, adding, "It's a big house."

The mansion was indeed big, she thought as she looked up at it. Big and ugly as if built by someone who wanted not to just impress but shock. There was nothing engaging about the structure. All she could hope was that it was more hospitable inside, since she didn't like old houses. As she stared at it, she feared coming here might have been a terrible mistake.

Alexa climbed out of her white SUV as the front door opened and her brother, Landon, came out to her. He looked so happy to see her that she shoved aside her misgivings.

"It is wonderful to see you," he said as he hugged her tightly. "Thank you so much for coming."

She drew back to study him, thinking how much she loved him. Sometimes she forgot how handsome and sweet he was. Their mother had called him her "little prince."

Both of them had adored Landon, but somehow he hadn't grown up spoiled.

If anything, he was too generous with his money and his love, Alexa thought, as Sierra appeared in the wide doorway.

"Welcome to Wellington Manor," Sierra said with a grand gesture. "That's what the locals call it and I think it fits the place. You're early. Supper's not quite ready. The others are either napping or in town for supplies but should be back any minute."

"The others?" Alexa asked her brother.

"We have friends helping get the house ready for guests," Landon said as he reached into the back of her vehicle for her suitcase. "Only one suitcase?" He looked disappointed as he hooked the strap of her bag over one shoulder.

"I travel light," she said with a smile and reluctantly let him lead her toward the mansion. She could feel tension between her brother and his new wife and suspected it hadn't been Sierra's idea to invite her to come for a stay.

She wondered whose idea it had been to have these friends help get the house ready for guests; after all Sierra and Landon had given up their honeymoon to come here and get started on the bed-and-breakfast.

As they walked toward the front entry, Alexa noticed something that hadn't registered minutes before. Her brother was rubbing his left arm.

"Did you hurt yourself?" she asked and saw him glance toward his wife before he answered.

"Just me being clumsy." He put his other arm around Alexa and smiled at his wife in the doorway. Sierra smiled back and disappeared into the house, leaving Alexa with the distinct impression that her brother was hiding something for Sierra's sake.

The moment she stepped into the house, she felt the cold. It instantly crept into her bones and made her shiver.

"It's a bit drafty," Sierra said, no doubt having witnessed Alexa's reaction.

She could see that both Sierra and Landon were defensive about the house. She fought not to show the effect it was having on her. The mansion had once been opulent, from the marble foyer to the huge sunken living room with its massive stone fireplace to the ornate stairway that swept upward to the floors above. Hallways ran from the living area like spider legs, disappearing in the dim light.

"Isn't it beautiful," Sierra gushed. "I just love it. Can't you see it as a bed-and-breakfast? Wait until you see the rest of it."

Alexa smiled at her sister-in-law's enthusiasm. The house had recently been cleaned but there was still a musty smell as if the rooms had been closed up—even though someone had been living here. Only a little light bled through the high leaded-stained-glass windows. Heavy velvet curtains hung next to the lower windows and while the glass had been recently cleaned, even the summer sun seemed to be having a hard time getting through.

"I'm sure you're tired after your long drive," her brother said, apparently wanting to talk to her alone. "Why don't I show you to your room."

"Oh, you'll want a tour first," Sierra said, sounding both surprised and annoyed at her husband's suggestion.

"I would love one later," Alexa said quickly. "Landon's right. I would like to freshen up first."

Sierra looked disappointed. "I've just been so excited to show you the house. My great-great-grandfather designed it, you know." She gave a little pout but said, "I guess I'll see how supper is coming instead. I think I hear the others pulling in now."

"I'd love to see it after we eat, thank you," Alexa said, relieved her sister-in-law hadn't insisted. She sensed Landon's need to talk to her, and whatever this was about, he hadn't wanted Sierra to hear.

He was quiet as he led her upstairs through what seemed like a maze of hallways before stopping at an end room. Opening the door, he stepped back to let her enter.

"Sierra got the room ready for you," he said, pride in his voice.

Alexa was reminded how much her brother loved his wife and how careful she had to be around Sierra so she didn't hurt his feelings. She knew she wasn't being fair. She barely knew the woman and chastised herself for not giving Sierra more of a chance.

"It's beautiful," she said as she entered the room. And it was.

The wood floors were buffed to a golden shine, and the huge canopy bed was adorned in white linens. An array of pillows were piled against the carved wooden headboard. An antique vanity stood against one wall, with two matching highboys and a loveseat and overstuffed chair on the other.

"The house came filled with furniture," Landon said. "There is even more up on the third floor. The last resident used that floor mostly for storage. The place really is huge, isn't it?"

He sounded nervous and while she was anxious to know why he'd gotten her here, she warned herself not to push.

"Sierra chose this room because of the view and the peace and quiet," Landon said. "It's the farthest from where the construction work is going on. We're remodeling some of the lower rooms that were built as servants' quarters."

"The view is wonderful," Alexa said as she stepped through the open French doors onto a small balcony. The land seemed vast and endless—just like the clear blue sky overhead. She'd never been to Montana before, but all the stories she'd heard about it seemed to be true. It really was amazing country. She could imagine what it must have been like when thousands of buffalo roamed it.

As she stared out, a cowboy on a horse came into view. Something in her froze. She stood transfixed as he rode from the stand of large cottonwood trees and into the sun and sage. For a moment she'd thought she'd conjured him up from her imagination because he looked so at home in the saddle with this landscape in the background. He wore jeans, boots, a red-checked western shirt and what she thought must be a Stetson resting on his longish, raven-black hair. A brown-and-white mutt of a dog ran along a few yards off to the side of his horse.

Alexa held her breath, wanting him to turn and look in her direction. She desperately needed to see his face.

Just when it appeared he would ride by without looking in her direction, he glanced up at her.

Chapter Two

Only two of the vehicles were still parked in front of the old Wellington mansion, the red sports car and the white SUV, Marshall Chisholm noted as he rode his horse by the house. The former street was no more than a narrow dirt lane with rows of huge, old cottonwood trees on each side.

The sports car had California plates, while the SUV was licensed out of Washington State. Neither rig looked as if it might belong to drug runners out of Canada hiding out here. The expensive sports car had a Montana State University sticker on the bumper. College students?

As he came out of the trees, he got his first close-up view of the house. He'd never paid much attention to the old place. Truth is, there was something about it that had always put him off. That and no doubt the stories he'd heard over the years.

Even up close, the mansion still didn't draw him. There was nothing in its design or the size of the place that made him want to stop and look. It was the three vehicles he'd seen here that had him curious. He wondered where the black SUV had gone.

As he circled around the place, he looked up at the blank windows, thinking he should probably just go knock at the huge front door and introduce himself as the only neighbor.

He was chewing on that idea when suddenly a young woman with long, dark, curly hair, wide violet eyes and the heart-shaped face of an angel appeared on a second-floor balcony.

But it was what he saw behind her that startled him. His horse suddenly snorted and jerked her head, eyes wild as she reared up. His western hat fell off as he fought to stay seated. He'd never seen the mare react like this before and knew he was lucky he hadn't been bucked off.

As he regained control of his mount, he glanced up again. The young woman was still standing there, but the image he'd seen behind her was gone.

She stood in the morning light, lithe, wraithlike against the darkness behind her.

A vision. Her hair floated around her face, falling about her shoulders in stark contrast to the white of the blouse she wore.

His dog, Angus, barked, making him start again. Everything about being here was making him jumpy as hell. He told himself he was letting his imagination run away with him. That and the stories he'd heard about the mansion—even though he'd always said he didn't believe a word of it.

"Hang on a minute, Angus," he said, glancing at the impatient mutt before looking back at the mansion window. The woman was gone.

Marshall felt a knot form in his belly as he continued to stare at the window for several long moments, trying to assure himself he hadn't imagined her any more than he'd imagined that other image standing behind her.

He wished to hell she would reappear just to prove to himself that she'd been real though.

You don't really believe that was a ghost you saw.

Of course, he didn't. But still there had been something about her, something ethereal, angelic. While what he'd seen behind her… He spurred his horse, chuckling at the strange trail his thoughts had taken. He didn't believe in ghosts or haunted houses. Or evil spirits.

But as warm as the summer morning felt with the sun hot on his back, he felt a chill.

"ALEXA, DID YOU HEAR what I said?"

She stepped back into the room, but she couldn't shake the rush of sensations she'd felt when she'd seen the handsome cowboy's face. A strange, wanton desire—and darkness.

Both frightened her by their intensity. She recalled how desperate she'd been to see his face. How she had needed him to look at her.

She shuddered, shocked by what she'd felt as much as by the force of it. Often she got sharp first impressions, but she'd convinced herself that other people got them too and often didn't recognize them. Everyone met people and in an instant decided if they liked them or not, and never questioned why.

Plain old intuition. She'd even convinced herself that her mother had probably merely been good at reading people, so of course her daughter had picked it up as well. Alexa wanted to believe that rather than the other possibility.

Since she was a girl she'd been haunted by the memory of waking to find her mother standing over her, telling her to look at something at the end of her bed.

Just the thought of it after all these years gave her chills, but she'd convinced herself that what she'd seen was nothing more than her imagination. Or part of a bad dream.

Unfortunately sometimes she felt things, sensed things, she didn't want to know about. She'd found it easier not to get too close to anyone. As long as she kept her distance and her defenses up, she could live blissfully oblivious about the people around her and their fates.

None of her earlier sensations, though, had ever been as powerful as what she'd felt when she'd seen the cowboy's face. Desire and darkness.

"Are you all right?" Landon asked as he touched her arm and she flinched.

"Yes." She shook her head as if she could shake off what she'd felt moments before. It had been so potent. "I'm just tired. It was a long drive."

"I hated to ask you to come...."

"No," she quickly reassured him. "I'd been wanting to come for a visit." Her brother reminded her of light. There was something so pure and innocent about him. He was loving and devoted, open and trusting.

Unlike her brother, she had never been open or trusting.

"You sounded strange on the phone," she said as she drew him over to the loveseat between the two highboys. "I was concerned." Alexa still worried why he had invited her here, almost pleading with her to come.

"I didn't mean to trouble you," he said, but looking at him she could tell something was wrong and said as much.

"Like I told you on the phone, it's the house."

"If you don't want to remodel it for a bed-and-breakfast then—"

"It's not that." He seemed to hesitate, his gaze locking with hers. "You're the only person I can tell this to who won't think I'm crazy. The house is trying to hurt me," he said dropping the words like stones into the room.

"What?" Alexa said, thinking she must have heard him wrong.

"You asked about my arm? A cabinet fell on me, but there have been other near misses since we got here."

"Landon, do you realize what you're saying?"

He nodded. "Do you remember when we were kids and Mother used to ask you if you saw…things that the rest of us couldn't see?"

As if she could forget. Alexa got up and moved to the open French doors again. There was no sign of the cowboy she'd seen earlier. "Landon, I've told you. I don't have the sight."

"Mother was convinced that you blocked it. That you were simply afraid of it but that if you let yourself—"

"Mother was wrong," she said, turning to face him. "This is all her fault," she continued with a wave of her hand that encompassed the house. "If not for her beliefs, then you would never be thinking that because of some isolated accidents…" The rest of her words died in her mouth as she saw her brother's crestfallen face. "This is why you got me here? To tell you whether or not this house is haunted?"

Her brother suddenly looked so young, so vulnerable, her heart nearly broke for him. "Something is wrong in this house," he said with obvious fear.

Before she could question him further, there was a knock at the door.

"Please don't say anything about this to my wife," he whispered hurriedly.

Alexa felt sick to her stomach. She couldn't believe this is why he'd gotten her here.

"So how do you like your room?" Sierra asked as she stuck her head into the doorway.

"It's lovely," Alexa told her, though still upset from her conversation with her brother. She was angry with him for getting her here under false pretenses and, at the same time, worried about him. Landon was scared. But he also had enough of their mother in him that he was prone to overreaction and flights of fantasy. His hasty marriage to a woman he barely knew and getting involved with this white elephant of a house were two perfect examples.

"You did a beautiful job," she said to Sierra. "I really think you have a talent for this."

Her sister-in-law beamed at the compliment. "I can't tell you what that means to me." She let out a pleased sigh. "Supper is ready. Afterwards I will give you a tour of the house. You really have to see it to appreciate how amazing it is."

Landon followed his wife out of the room, hesitating only long enough to say to his sister, "We'll talk later."

As Alexa stepped out into the hallway, she felt a winterlike draft that stole her breath. She suppressed a shudder as she saw her brother watching her and realized Sierra was also intently focused on her.

Of course her brother would have told his wife everything about his family—Alexa included.

"HAS ANYONE HEARD ANYTHING about the people who are staying at the old Wellington place?" Marshall asked as casually as possible during supper at the Chisholm ranch that evening.

While he and his five brothers all had their own houses, they still had breakfast most mornings at the Chisholm Cattle Company main house—and were always expected for supper unless they were out of town *or* dead.

Their new stepmother, Emma, had a hard-and-fast rule about them being at the table on time, showered and shaved and without any manure on their boots. So tonight they were all seated at the table, his father, Hoyt, stepmother, Emma, and his five brothers, Dawson, Colton, Zane, Logan and Tanner.

"I heard something in town about a bunch of hippies moving into it," Colton said as he helped himself to more roast beef from the huge platter in front of him. "You want Halley to check on it?" Deputy Halley Robinson was Colton's fiancée.

Marshall chuckled at the hippie remark. Anyone from California with relatively long hair was considered a hippie in this part of Montana. The word covered a lot of territory.

He thought of the woman he'd seen at the window. "I think they might have bought the place."

"That's news to me," his father said, frowning. "I'd have known if it had come on the market. I've been trying to buy it for years and was told the family wasn't interested. Since the old woman who lived there died, the place has been tied up in the estate."

"I wonder then if the people I saw over there might be related to the original owner," Marshall mused.

"What is your interest anyway?" Zane asked, studying him.

"Just curious," Marshall said, feeling all eyes at the table on him. He was a terrible liar and they all knew it. "I can see the place from my house. I noticed activity over there, three cars, and just wondered what was going on. As I was driving in for supper, I passed a local hardware truck headed out that way with a lot of supplies in the back."

"You think they're remodeling it?" Hoyt said. "I can't imagine anyone wanting to live in such a huge place. Unless they have something else in mind for it."

"Are you talking about that old mansion north of here?" Emma asked. "I'd hate to have to heat that place in the winter. Why, it must have thirty bedrooms."

"I heard the old woman who lived there last stayed in just a small part of the house, boarding up the rest," Hoyt said, still frowning.

"Was it once a hotel or something?" Emma asked.

"That might have been the original plan," Hoyt said, "but the community of Wellington died when the railroad came through twenty miles to the south. I still can't believe anyone has moved in there with the idea of staying."

In the silence that followed, Tanner said, "The place has a dark history. I had some friends who went out there one night. They said they heard a baby crying and when they left they were chased by a pickup truck that disappeared at the edge of town. Just disappeared."

"I've heard stories about the Phantom Truck," Logan said.

Emma laughed. "Oh, posh. You aren't trying to tell me that the place is haunted or something silly like that." She glanced around the table. "Hoyt?"

Her husband sighed. "Let's just say that if a building can be haunted, it would be that one. The Wellingtons had their share of tragedies."

"Ghosts are said to have been born out of tragedy," Logan added and grinned mischievously.

Emma shook her head and turned to Marshall. "What do these people who have moved in look like?"

"I only saw one of them," he said, then remembered the image he'd seen behind the woman and felt a chill snake up his spine. "She *could* have been a ghost."

Emma shot him a disapproving look. "I'm asking if they seem like decent enough people and if they do, I think as their only neighbor you should go over there, introduce yourself and be neighborly. I'll bake something for you to take." She was already on her feet.

Hoyt was shaking his head. "You might want to get the lay of the land before you do that. Who knows who might have moved in there? We've had trouble with drug runners from Canada, escaped prisoners from Deer Lodge, criminals crossing the border through some barbed-wire fence and heading for the first house they see. Until you know who you're dealing with—"

"Hoyt!" Emma chastised. "I'm sure all those instances were rare. I've read the local paper. There is hardly ever any crime up here. And Marshall is no fool. He'll go over and meet them and make up his own mind. I'm sure they're fine people if they're remodeling the place and determined to live here."

They all loved Emma's positive attitude, no matter how naïve. But Marshall found himself poking at his food, his appetite gone as he remembered how his horse had spooked—not to mention his own reaction to what he'd seen just inside that balcony.

SUPPER AT WELLINGTON MANOR was served in the warm kitchen at a long, old table with mismatched chairs and dishes. The casserole that Carolina had fixed was delicious, and Alexa did her best to relax.

Carolina was a twenty-something, soft-spoken, pretty woman with blond hair, green eyes and porcelain skin. Her father, Sierra had said by way of introduction, had made his fortune in the hotel business. Carolina seemed shy and clearly embarrassed by Sierra's introduction.

Her husband, Archer, was boisterous and big, a bodybuilder who apparently had been a football star until an injury had sidelined him. His father was a producer in Hollywood, his mother a lawyer.

The other couple, Gigi and Devlin, seemed cut from the same expensive cloth, both with parents who had retired to Palm Desert, California. Gigi's long white-blond hair was pulled up in a ponytail, making her blue eyes seem even larger, her tiny nose all the more cute. A slender, athletic-looking young woman, she was in her twenties but could have passed for sixteen with her sweet, innocent face.

Her husband, Devlin, was a beach-boy blond with blue eyes. He laughed when Sierra introduced him as a rich kid whose parents owned a couple of vineyards in northern California. He'd had some wine shipped from home, which he poured with enthusiasm.

The lone wolf of the group was Jayden Farrell, whose father was an unemployed actor in Los Angeles, according to Sierra. Unlike the others, he was thirty-something and apparently hadn't been raised privileged. But he was as movie-star handsome as the others, maybe even more so because there was intelligence behind his blue eyes that Alexa found both appealing and disturbing.

Not only that, Jayden also seemed to set himself apart from this group, watching them almost with amusement. Alexa doubted the rest of them had noticed the disdain for them that she glimpsed in his gaze. What was this single man doing here with these married couples, especially when she sensed he didn't like them?

As the group around the table talked and joked, she and Jayden remained silent, she noted. She listened to them talk about their many university degrees, extended European trips and the benefits of growing up in sunny California.

None seemed to have professions, at least no jobs that kept them from helping their friends Sierra and Landon with their mansion, Jayden again being the exception. He'd made a point of saying that he'd studied business finance and would have to leave this fall to pursue his career.

The others seemed to see this Montana

bed-and-breakfast venture as a lark, a great adventure, something to tell their friends about when they returned to their real lives. Jayden was more serious, which made Alexa all the more curious about his motives for being here.

Through all the laughter and camaraderie during the meal, Alexa found herself studying her brother. If she hadn't known Landon so well, she might have thought he felt at ease with the assembled group, even though his roots were nothing like theirs. It was clear that Sierra had come from their world, though, rather than the one Alexa and Landon had grown up in. This made the reporter in Alexa curious, since Sierra had said she had been raised by a single mother in what she made sound like the Los Angeles projects.

Something was definitely wrong with that story, Alexa thought as she watched Sierra interacting with her friends. There was a gaiety to their stories. These young people had no worries—unlike her brother who seemed to be working hard not to show his.

Alexa also sensed tension within the group but couldn't pinpoint exactly where it was coming from. All she knew for sure was that her brother's forced merriment tonight didn't fool her for a minute. If only their mother was here. Tallulah Cross would have sized up this bunch in an instant and known exactly what was going on.

Alexa hated that she felt bombarded by conflicting sensations in this house. Something was trying to break through the wall she'd built to keep these kinds of sensations out. For years, she'd feared she'd lied as much to herself as she had to her mother and brother. She felt things, things she didn't want to feel. But if she truly had her mother's gift, she was terrified of it, didn't know how to use it and had done everything she could to block it for so long that she had no control over it.

Coming here had been a mistake and yet even as she thought about leaving, she knew she couldn't abandon her brother. Not when she knew something was wrong in this house. He'd said he'd already had a series of accidents. What if he was right about something—or someone—wanting him out of the mansion?

By the time supper was over, Archer had the flushed face of a man who'd consumed more wine than anyone else. Sierra was in a friendly debate with Carolina and Gigi about the best sushi restaurants they'd ever gone to outside of California. Archer and Devlin excused themselves, saying they were going to try to catch the baseball game on television.

Alexa rose to help with the dishes.

"It's Gigi and Landon's turn to do the dishes," Sierra insisted. "Come on. I want to show you the house."

"Go on," Landon said. "I'll catch up with you later."

Alexa had hoped to talk to her brother after supper and wished the two of them could have done the dishes together, but Sierra was determined to show her the house.

"You have to see this," she said as they passed through the huge living area. She pushed open two large carved wooden doors. "The library," she announced with a grand gesture. The books on the shelves had been moved and stacked as if someone had gone through them, the thick layer of dust that coated the room disturbed.

"We have so much to do before the house is restored," she said. "But I love this room and can't wait to get to it."

Closing the doors, Sierra led her down a hallway, pointing out the servants' quarters, most of the rooms empty except for one that Jayden was using. In another wing there was a music room with an old piano, and finally the ballroom.

All of the rooms looked as if a little work had been done in them. Alexa had the feeling, though, that not much was getting done—at least from what she'd seen so far.

"Let's take the back stairs," Sierra said and led Alexa up to a wing of the second floor.

Alexa felt a little turned around and said as much.

Sierra laughed. "It does get confusing. That's why I ask that you not go exploring on your own. It is too easy to get hurt, and who knows how long it would be before anyone found you?" She laughed as if delighted by the size of this place.

Alexa thought of her brother's accidents and wondered how long it had been before he'd been found.

"We are in the north wing. Your room is in the east wing, Gigi and Dev have a room on the west wing, Carolina and Archer are on the south wing, Jayden's on the first floor in the servants' quarters. His choice," she added quickly. "We decided we might as well stretch out and have our own space."

She remembered at supper how she'd felt the others occasionally studying her with interest. She realized with a start that Sierra had probably told her friends about Landon's sister's "sight." She groaned inwardly at the thought that everyone in this house would be watching her now.

"Jayden's kind of a loner."

Alexa mentioned her surprise that he had wanted to be here with three couples, as Sierra led her along a long, dark hallway.

"He's one of the gang," Sierra said. "I guess I was a little surprised too that he came with us. But we all loved him the moment we met him. Isn't the house in great shape for how old it is?"

"Some relative of yours lived here most recently?" Alexa asked.

"My great cousin lived here until she died," Sierra said. "I never knew her. Most of the rooms were closed off while she lived here. She stayed in one of the maids' rooms downstairs, where Jayden is on the first floor." She chuckled again. "The old maid in the maids' quarters. It's pretty funny. I doubt she even came up to these rooms."

Alexa couldn't help but wonder why Jayden preferred one of the small rooms for maids rather than the opulence—not to mention the views—of an upstairs bedroom. Maybe he didn't hold himself apart only at supper.

As they left the catacomb of rooms and hallways to return to the main hall, she saw that the kitchen was empty. Gigi and Landon had finished the dishes. Alexa couldn't wait to get him alone to talk to him again.

"Do you know where I can find Landon?" she asked.

Sierra shrugged. "I'll tell him if I see him before bedtime."

She got the feeling Sierra had no intention of telling him. "Thank you for the tour."

"My pleasure, although I do wish you had waited until the house was done before coming for a visit," Sierra said.

"Landon asked me to come now."

Her sister-in-law raised a brow. "Did he? I wish he'd discussed it with me first." She smiled and let out a small, humorless laugh. "I guess it isn't that big of a deal. I just wanted everything to be perfect the first time you saw it."

With that, Sierra gave a wave and disappeared down a hallway.

Alexa looked around the huge living room, thinking that her brother had made a mistake calling her. Not only had he upset his new bride, but also, she thought, spotting a Ouija board on the coffee table in front of the huge fireplace, he'd called the wrong person.

Landon would have been much better off trying to reach their mother.

Chapter Three

Sheriff McCall Crawford knew it had been impulsive and no doubt a fool's errand, especially coming here after work. It was dark and late as she pulled into the parking lot at the state mental hospital.

Her husband, Luke, had tried to dissuade her, but after the call she'd gotten from the doctor, she had to make sure for herself—not to mention for the safety of the Chisholm family.

"Why did you fail to mention the extent of Aggie Wells's alcoholism?" the doctor had chided her on the phone when he'd caught her at work earlier. "We almost lost her last night. Had we known of her problem, we would have eased her off the alcohol with the use of drugs—"

"Doctor, I'm sorry. I was completely unaware that Aggie Wells had an alcohol addiction. Are you sure she wasn't…faking it?"

"You can't be serious! One look at this woman and it would be apparent to anyone that she was most certainly not 'faking it,' as you so delicately put it. A blood test confirmed that the woman is an alcoholic. We don't assume anything around *here*."

McCall had felt confused. "Are you sure we're talking about the same patient?"

"Agatha Wells."

Still something was wrong and McCall felt it.

Now as she climbed out of her car and started into the state mental hospital, she had to see for herself what Aggie Wells was up to. Aggie hadn't exhibited any signs of alcoholism when she'd been in the Whitehorse jail over the past few months.

The doctor didn't know how smart and manipulative this woman was. Nor was he aware of the extremes Aggie would go to in an attempt to get what she wanted. McCall did though, since she'd been the one to arrest her.

A former insurance investigator, Aggie Wells had taken pride in exposing anyone who tried to defraud the company she worked for. But something had happened on one of her first cases, more than thirty years before. It had been the life insurance case of Laura Chisholm, first wife of Hoyt Chisholm, of the Chisholm Cattle Company.

Aggie hadn't been able to accept that Laura Chisholm's drowning had been accidental. And while she couldn't prove it, she also wouldn't give up. When Hoyt's second wife was killed in a horseback riding accident, Aggie again tried to prove murder. Failing that, she'd only become more obsessed. A few years later, when he'd remarried once again and his wife had disappeared, Aggie Wells was determined the woman had been murdered—to the extent it was now believed that Aggie had killed his third wife herself to prove Hoyt Chisholm a murderer by framing him.

Hoyt had gone years after that without marrying, turning all of his attention to raising the six boys he'd adopted. A few months ago he'd met Emma McDougal at a cattlemen's convention in Denver and fallen so hard, that the two ran off to Vegas and married.

Even though she'd lost her job at the insurance company because of her obsession with the Hoyt Chisholm case, Aggie Wells had come back into his life, determined that he wouldn't get the chance to kill another wife. She'd bugged his house, tried to frame him for the murder of his third wife, after her body had mysteriously turned up, and she'd abducted Emma, his new bride.

Fortunately, McCall had stopped her before Aggie could harm Emma. After taking Aggie's statement following her arrest, she claimed that Hoyt Chisholm's first wife, Laura, was still alive, and it was Laura who had killed his other two wives and would soon kill wife number four unless the sheriff didn't set her free to save Emma.

After hearing Aggie's testimony, the county attorney had finally ordered a mental evaluation to see if Aggie Wells was fit to stand trial, and sent her to the state hospital.

"I'm here to see Aggie Wells," McCall said as she showed her identification at the front desk of the hospital. "Dr. Barsness is expecting me."

"The third door on the right," the receptionist said, pointing down a long hallway.

At her knock, a male voice on the other side told her to come in. A balding, short man looked up from his untidy desk as McCall entered the small office. Dr. Barsness looked busy and irritated. It was clear he thought her visit was a waste of his time and hers. She thought he might be right.

But if Aggie Wells had a drinking problem so extreme that she'd almost died from withdrawal at the mental hospital, then McCall wanted to know why none of them had suspected it during her stay in the Whitehorse jail. Unless Aggie had somehow talked someone at the jail into getting her alcohol behind McCall's back. And if that was the case, the sheriff was bound and determined to find out.

"I won't take but a few minutes of your time," she said as the doctor got to his feet with a heavy sigh. "I just want to see Aggie for myself."

With a shake of his head, he led her down the hallway through several locked doors into a noisy ward and finally to a room at the end of a hall.

He opened the door with a key. "Miss Wells? You have company."

McCall looked into the narrow room. The only furniture was a bed bolted to the wall. A figure lay in the bed, covered with a blanket, face to the wall in a fetal position.

McCall remembered the woman she'd arrested for abducting Emma Chisholm and suspicion of murder. Aggie was a tall, slender, attractive woman. Also a very intelligent woman with a lot of resources at her disposal and enough knowledge about illegal things to make her dangerous.

"Aggie?" McCall asked as she stepped in. The room had an odd smell to it and she was reminded of a homeless man her deputies had put up in a cell for the night last winter. He'd had that smell. *"Aggie?"*

The woman in the bed rolled over and squinted. "What?"

McCall took a step back, shocked by what she saw. Alcohol and a hard life had ravaged this woman's face, making her appear years older than she was. "You aren't Aggie Wells."

"Yes, I am. My name is Agatha Wells," the woman said. "I used to work as an insurance investigator...."

The sheriff turned to the doctor. "This is not the prisoner I sent you for a mental evaluation. This woman has obviously been coached. Where is Aggie Wells?"

Even as she asked it, McCall was reaching for her cell phone. If Aggie Wells was on the loose, then she had to warn the Chisholms—especially Emma.

HER MOTHER WAS ON HER MIND as Alexa got ready for bed. Since Tallulah Cross had died a year ago, Alexa's greatest fear had been that her mother would try to contact her from the beyond. To her relief, she hadn't. But in this house she felt vulnerable so it was no wonder she was thinking of her mother, she told herself. She hadn't been able to talk to her brother again. According to Sierra, there was some sort of water leak in the basement and he and the other men had gone down to fix it.

Sierra had said that the "girls" were going to build a fire and have a few drinks before bed. Alexa had excused herself, feigning exhaustion from her long drive. She *was* exhausted but not from the drive. She told herself it was from being in this house with all these people and worrying about her brother.

The truth, she finally admitted when she reached her room, was that her brother was right. This house had a dark history that had been coming at her like a battering ram. While she couldn't say what it was exactly, she could feel the unrest of a house that had known its share of tragedy.

As Alexa turned on a light, chasing the

dark shadows back into the far corners of the room, she fought the urge to pack and get away from here as fast as possible. She didn't want to know what was going on in this house. She wanted to go back to her life in Spokane, where no one knew that her mother had been Tallulah Cross, the fortune-teller and infamous psychic.

But she knew she couldn't go anywhere tonight. Tomorrow, she would try to talk her brother into leaving here. If she could get him away from the house…

Her head ached as she stepped through the open French doors to the balcony and looked out on the peaceful landscape. She breathed in the sweet, summer's night air and tried to calm herself. Landon would never leave his wife without reason. Which meant Alexa couldn't leave until she knew that reason or was sure that her brother was safe.

These accidents he'd been having—wasn't it possible that's all they were?

Of course it was. Her brother could be overreacting because of their mother's profession and his DNA. While he apparently hadn't inherited what he and their mother called the "gift," he still had the same genes.

Alexa started to move away from the

window when she saw a light in the distance. Another house. Was that where the cowboy lived whom she'd seen earlier?

At a sound outside, she quickly extinguished the lamp. Two figures moved through the deep shadows of the trees out to what appeared to be a pond. She could see the faint moonlight shimmering on a portion of the water's surface through the thick-leafed branches of the trees.

She could make out the shapes of the figures. A man and a woman walked side by side, not touching and staying in the shadow of the trees. Was it only her imagination that they avoided the moonlight because they didn't want to be seen together?

Standing in a dark corner of the balcony, Alexa watched the two stop under a tree. They were talking, facing each other. She couldn't hear their words—only read their body language.

They were arguing. She wondered if it was Archer and his wife. Carolina hadn't seemed happy with all the wine he'd consumed at supper.

But as she watched, she realized the man was taller than Archer and slimmer. Jayden. The argument was growing louder and more violent. Alexa caught snatches of the conversation.

"Stop worrying…no reason to panic."

"You smug bastard."

"Keep your voice down."

"Don't tell me what… I don't know why I ever…"

She heard what sounded like a slap, then another, followed by a small cry. The woman started to leave, but Jayden pulled her back. The two dark figures melted together and the night grew silent again.

Who had the woman been? Alexa hadn't been able to recognize her voice from the distance and hearing only snatches of the conversation. Gigi? Carolina?

With a start, Alexa reminded herself there were three women in this house—all of them about the same size—and all blond.

The woman she'd just seen in Jayden's arms could have been Sierra—her brother's wife.

MARSHALL HAD A HELL OF A time getting to sleep after he got the call from his father about Aggie Wells being on the loose again.

"Are you sure you don't want me to come

spend the night at the main house?" he'd asked after hearing that no one knew where Aggie was. The woman was believed to be a killer. She'd abducted his stepmother and done her best to frame his father for murder. Marshall couldn't believe that she'd somehow not just gotten away, but paid some woman to pretend to be her at the mental hospital.

"Don't worry," his father had said. "The doors are locked and the shotgun is beside my bed. Emma and I are fine. The sheriff has a deputy parked outside tonight."

Still, Marshall had felt restless after the conversation with his father. Aggie Wells was crazy. Who knew what a crazy woman would do next?

He'd stood for a long time just looking toward the east and the faint glow of golden light from Wellington Manor.

"Speaking of crazy," he'd said to his dog, Angus, remembering his earlier impressions. He'd assured himself that the woman he'd seen was real and what he'd seen standing behind the woman at the window had been a trick of the light, no more than a shadow, and that tomorrow morning he was going to ride over there and introduce himself. Emma had insisted on baking a batch of her gingersnap cookies to take before he'd left the house earlier.

He'd finally gone to bed and felt as if he'd only just drifted off when he was awakened with a jolt. Lying in bed listening, he wasn't sure what had brought him out of his sleep so suddenly. He glanced at the clock, surprised it was only an hour or so before daybreak, then glanced toward the open window and darkness beyond—and saw his dog standing there, looking out, the hair on the dog's back sticking straight up. Angus let out a low growl.

"What is it, boy?" Marshall whispered as he slipped out of the bed and padded quietly over to the window. A sliver of moon hung on the edge of the horizon, golden among the canopy of stars. The breeze was scented with the smells of August, golden grasses heavy and ripe with grain.

He loved this time of year because he knew how fleeting it was. Montana was a place of seasons that changed with little notice. One day could be hot and beautiful, the next the temperature would drop and that season would be over. Or after an unusually long winter, the snow would suddenly melt and the air would smell of spring.

His thoughts surprised him because there was almost regret in them. Another summer almost gone. He could feel his life slipping away. Part of the problem, he knew, was that three of his brothers had fallen in love and were talking marriage. He hadn't been aware of a time when all six of them weren't sowing their oats, the wild sons of Hoyt Chisholm.

"I don't see anything," he told the dog and started to head back to bed, no longer concerned about what had awakened him.

The scream made him spin around to the window again. He realized it was what must have awakened him and had Angus on alert.

His gaze went to the Wellington mansion, but all he saw was darkness at first. Then a flash of white caught his eye. A woman was running across the pasture toward his house.

Marshall felt a chill wrap around his neck and tighten at the sight of the same ghostlike woman he'd seen earlier in the second-story window of the mansion.

Unable to move at first, he stood watching her approach. She ran as if the devil himself were at her heels and yet he could see no one, nothing, chasing her.

Hell, he wasn't even sure *she* was real. Maybe he was just dreaming her.

But Angus thought she was real. He let out a bark and tore downstairs as the woman turned to look behind her, stumbled and almost fell and another terrified scream burst from her throat.

Pulling on his jeans, Marshall raced downstairs and out onto the porch as she emerged from the field and into his yard. He bolted down the porch steps as she stumbled and fell on the patch of grass in front of his house.

She was breathing hard, huge gasps and sobs emitting from her, her body quaking from exertion and whatever had her so terrified. Angus had stopped partway out into the yard and stood as if frozen in midstep, a low growl coming from his throat.

"Stay!" Marshall ordered the dog as the woman staggered to her feet. She wore a thin, white nightgown, her lush body silhouetted against the moon and starlight and more beautiful than he thought possible.

As he rushed to her, she looked up, but her eyes had a strange emptiness to them, as if whatever she was seeing wasn't really there.

Marshall wasn't even sure she was real

until she fell into his arms and he felt the weight and warmth of the flesh-and-blood woman.

THE NIGHTMARES HAD ALWAYS been waiting for her the moment Alexa closed her eyes. They had terrified her when she was a child. As she got older, she'd come to accept them, telling herself they weren't real.

But of course they were. Her mother knew, that's why Alexa had often found Tallulah standing over her at night as if gazing at the nightmares like a horror film on television.

"I'm always watching over you," her mother used to say, the words giving her no comfort.

"Why don't you wake me up and hold me like my father used to?" she'd wanted to know. When her father had touched her, she had always awakened from the horrors of her dream.

"They're *your* nightmares, Alexa. You must learn to control them. You have the power—if you choose to use it." Her mother would give her that look that said she suspected Alexa had lied about not having the gift.

Just as the nightmare would end the

moment her father awakened her, this one ended the moment the cowboy took her in his arms.

Alexa looked up into his face, felt the lingering effects of her nightmare, the exertion of her run across the pasture toward the only light she'd seen, the shock of finding herself in the cowboy's arms and fainted.

When she came to, she was lying on the cowboy's couch with a cool, damp washcloth on her forehead. His dog, the one she'd seen with him earlier that day, was sitting in front of her, staring at her.

She sat up abruptly, making her head swim, the blanket he'd covered her with falling to her lap.

The dog growled.

She quickly pulled the blanket back up over her thin cotton nightgown, aware of how naked she was beneath it and how big his dog was.

"Don't let Angus scare you," the cowboy said as he came into the room. "I told him to watch you while I got you something to drink." He had a glass of water in one hand and a bottle of beer in the other. He must have realized her fear wasn't just of the dog because he stopped midway into the room.

"I thought you might like some water," he said and stepped forward to offer her the glass. He'd put on a shirt and boots since she'd last seen him. She recalled the feel of his broad, warm, bare chest before she fainted. Just as he must remember the sheerness of her nightgown.

She felt her face heat with embarrassment. She wasn't overly modest but she did hate anyone knowing about her nightmares, and she wasn't in the habit of visiting neighbors half-naked.

"Or you're welcome to the beer," he said. "I don't know about you, but I could use a drink."

She couldn't help but smile at his gentle manner and kind, almost embarrassed, expression. She accepted the glass of water with a "Thank you," and took a sip as he sat down in a chair across from her.

"I see you've met Angus," the cowboy said. "He seems pretty taken with you. I apologize for his manners. But he only stares at people he likes."

She could tell he was trying to make her feel at ease. It was working.

He held his bottle of beer as he looked at

her, then as if remembering it in his hand, he took a long drink.

"I'm glad to see you're feeling better," he said, wiping his mouth with the back of his hand self-consciously and she realized she was smiling at him again. There was just something about him. She loved the dark sheen of his longish straight, black hair, the deep, rich hues of his equally dark eyes. His skin was a warmer mocha than her own— hers descending from Gypsies, his, she guessed, from a Native American mother or father.

It surprised her that she wasn't the one feeling self-conscious, since she had on less clothing then he had and had obviously awakened him in the middle of the night, dragging him into one of her nightmares. And yet she didn't. She felt strangely safe here with him. Even the house felt inviting. Is that why she'd run to him in her nightmare?

She'd never been able to remember anything about her nightmares when she'd awakened and had always been glad of that.

"You need to try to remember your dreams," her mother had said many times. "They signify something important either from your past or your future. Stop being afraid of them."

That only had made Alexa more terrified of the nightmares, since she didn't want to see into the future. It also had made her all the more determined to keep them from her conscious mind. She'd become very good at it. Like tonight. She had no memory of what had sent her out into the night.

"I'm sorry. I must have frightened you," she said as he took another drink of his beer and she realized that he was shaken by what had happened. "I must have been screaming?"

He nodded.

Alexa had often awakened in the middle of a bloodcurdling scream. The horror and pain in the sound had made her all the more terrified. What in her subconscious could frighten her so much? She could only imagine, given the kinds of things her mother used to tell her about the people she read fortunes for.

"Bad dream?"

She nodded, took a deep breath and let it out slowly as she felt her strength coming back into her. The nightmares took something out of her. When she was younger, she sleepwalked a lot, waking up in strange, frightening places.

It had been years, though, since she'd taken off in her sleep. She didn't need to think hard to figure out what had caused the relapse as she glanced out the window and saw Wellington Manor in the distance. The sun was starting to come up, the horizon a fiery red, shafts of light streaking up into the big, dark sky above it.

She turned to look at the cowboy again. "You don't happen to have another one of those beers, do you? I think I could use something stronger myself."

He chuckled as he got to his feet and took her water glass, returning with a bottle of beer and a clean glass. She shook her head when he offered her the glass and noticed his large, callused hands as he twisted off the cap and handed her the cold bottle.

Alexa took a swallow. She couldn't remember the last time she'd had a beer. Especially just before daybreak. It tasted better than anything she could remember ever drinking. "It's wonderful."

He smiled at that as he sat down again. She could see that he wanted to ask her about the nightmare, but was either too polite or too shy. Or maybe too afraid of the answer.

"I suppose we should introduce ourselves,"

she said, thinking this had to be the strangest way she'd ever met a man. "Alexa Cross."

"Marshall Chisholm," he said, leaning forward to shake her hand. "Nice to meet you." His rough hand felt surprisingly warm even though it was the one he'd been holding his beer bottle in. His dark eyes held that same warmth.

She took another sip of her beer and said into the silence, "I'm a reporter from Spokane visiting my brother, Landon. His wife, Sierra, inherited the Wellington house. He and some of their friends are helping her remodel it."

It was the reporter in her that had her sizing up the situation in as few words as possible, known in journalism as the "nut graph."

Taking her example, he said, "My family runs the Chisholm Cattle Company. I saw you over at the house when I went for a horseback ride yesterday. You were standing on one of the upstairs balconies. I thought you were a ghost."

Alexa laughed. "Then I can well imagine what you thought when you heard me screaming and saw me running across your field."

SHE HAD A GREAT LAUGH AND Marshall found himself relaxing as the sun came up behind her through the window and they drank their beers.

He waited, thinking she might tell him about what had sent her out into the night like that, but she didn't. There was something almost exotic about her, the wild, curly dark hair, those amazing violet eyes that pulled him in like a well-thrown lasso, that heart-shaped face. He couldn't help but remember the body he'd seen in the moonlight and starlight.

She was beautiful and she'd ended up on his doorstep. He felt privileged and smiled to himself when he saw that Angus seemed just as smitten with her.

He could have warned the dog though. There was something inaccessible about Alexa Cross. He recognized it because he was like that himself. He was no stranger to the walls that people built to protect themselves. But last night he'd felt as if a part of those walls had come crashing down when she'd stumbled into his arms.

"I should get back before I'm missed," she said as she finished her beer.

He got up to take her empty bottle. "I'll drive you." He could tell she didn't want to put him to any trouble but also didn't want to make the trek back across the pasture. "I've also got some clothes that might fit you...."

"Thank you. I'd appreciate that."

He left her on the couch with Angus watching over her and went upstairs to rummage in his bureau, returning to find her still wrapped in the blanket he'd put over her earlier. As he handed her a flannel shirt, a pair of his jeans, a belt and some knitted slippers someone had given him for Christmas, he pointed to the bathroom off the kitchen.

"I'm sorry, but the clothes are going to swallow you," he said as she, still in the blanket, padded barefoot to the bathroom. "I apologize. That's the smallest I could find."

She came out of the bathroom a few minutes later and handed him his blanket, now neatly folded, along with his jeans and belt. He couldn't help but smile at the sight of her. She'd rolled up the sleeves of his flannel shirt but the hem dropped past her knees.

The knitted slippers were a little floppy but would work. He knew her bare feet had to be sore after running through the pasture the way she had. Just a bad dream? That was a hell of a long way to run in the middle of the night because of a bad dream.

"I couldn't keep the jeans up," she said.

"But I will borrow your shirt and slippers. I'll see that you get them back though."

"No hurry," he said, looking forward to seeing her again, even though he'd been around long enough to know that there was something going on with this woman, more than bad dreams.

Chapter Four

The house was quiet as Alexa let herself in. She'd feared that the front door might be locked. Or that someone in the house had heard Marshall's truck as he dropped her off.

But as she stepped inside, she heard no sound of life. It wouldn't have surprised her to learn that the occupants weren't early risers. She hurriedly mounted the stairs and walked the long hallway to her room, making as little noise as possible.

Once inside her room, she finally let out the breath she'd been holding. The last thing she wanted was to have to explain where she'd been or why some neighboring cowboy had brought her home at daybreak with the smell of beer on her breath.

She smiled at the thought of how her brother would react—let alone Sierra—as she started to take off the shirt Marshall had lent her. She caught a whiff of his male scent and slowly lifted the sleeve to her face, breathing him in, her smile widening at the memory of the sweet, bashful cowboy.

Reminding herself of her first instincts about him, the wanton desire and the darkness, she quickly stripped off the shirt, her nightgown and his slippers and headed for the shower. She couldn't explain either sensation she felt. But standing under the spray she let herself admit how much she'd enjoyed the handsome cowboy, his home and even his dog.

Later, after she'd dressed in a blouse and skirt and sandals, Alexa made her way downstairs to the empty kitchen. She'd barely gotten a pot of coffee going when Sierra walked in wearing a robe and slippers. She looked as if she'd just woken up and Alexa couldn't help but notice that her eyes were red and puffy as if she'd been crying.

She was reminded of last night and the fight Jayden had had with one of the women from this house out near the pond.

"Good morning," she said to her sister-in-law.

As Alexa handed her a cup of coffee, Sierra gave a small grunt and dropped into a kitchen chair. Alexa joined her at the table, cradling her cup in her hands and watching Sierra through the steam.

Was it possible her brother had gotten her here under the pretext that the house was haunted and trying to hurt him, but something else entirely was going on and he knew it? Or at least suspected it?

After a few sips of coffee, Sierra seemed to stir. She blinked as if only then aware of Alexa's presence. "So how did you sleep?"

"Fine." She could feel Sierra's blue eyes boring into her. Did she know about her nightmare last night or her excursion to the neighbor's?

"I put a down comforter on your bed. Was it warm enough?"

"It was perfect."

Sierra nodded and took another drink of her coffee, seemingly content with the answers, but Alexa could tell that something was bothering her. What had made her eyes puffy and red this morning?

Alexa got up to refill their cups. When she came back to the table, Sierra was pulling a tissue from her robe pocket and blowing her nose. "Allergies," she said when she saw Alexa looking at her.

Feeling relieved, she started to fill Sierra's

coffee cup, but her sister-in-law quickly put her hand over the top to stop her.

"Can you read coffee grounds?"

Alexa felt as if she'd been slapped. She'd suspected Landon had told his wife not only about their mother, but also his suspicions about her as well. Now there was no doubt, was there?

"No."

Sierra looked disappointed. "What about tea leaves?"

"I'm sorry, but I don't read anything but printed words," Alexa said as she refilled her own coffee cup, then motioned to Sierra's, who reluctantly moved her hand to let her fill it. She was trembling with indignation as she took the pot back over to the counter. She knew she shouldn't be so upset, but she couldn't help it.

No one in Spokane knew about her mother or the world she'd come from, and Alexa liked it that way. She had made a point of putting that life behind her the moment she'd left home. Now she felt betrayed by her brother and hurt. She should have realized that he didn't have the same kind of abhorrence about growing up with a fortune-teller for a mother that she did. His friends probably found it amusing, his background unique.

"Landon said you were touchy about your powers and didn't like using them, but I thought since we were family…" Sierra said, pouting.

Powers? Sierra made it sound as if Alexa was a superhero. She started to tell her that there were no "powers" and that knowing too much was a curse. Just like knowing that Sierra was the wrong woman for her brother. But Carolina and Gigi came into the kitchen, followed close behind by Archer and Devlin. As Jayden came in and plopped down in a chair across from Sierra, Alexa watched the three women for a reaction.

Sierra didn't even bother to look up. She was still pouting. Carolina began to pour all of the men coffee as Gigi made herself a piece of toast.

Whoever had been down by the pond last night with Jayden must have patched up things with him. But he'd been with one of them and Alexa had seen how intimate the argument—and the making up—had been.

One of these women was cheating on her husband.

But which one?

With Landon running scared, Alexa feared what she'd witnessed last night was at the heart of what her brother had to fear in this house.

EMMA CHISHOLM SAT ACROSS the table from the sheriff, telling herself she wasn't all that surprised that Aggie Wells had managed to get away. Next to her, Hoyt was trying hard to contain his anger. He was scared. She was too.

"I just don't understand how this could have happened," he said to the sheriff.

"That's what we're trying to figure out. Aggie managed to make the switch before the van reached the hospital. That means she had help."

"Who?" Hoyt demanded.

"We don't know yet," the sheriff said.

"This homeless woman who Aggie substituted for herself, she's admitted that she was paid to pretend to be Aggie?" Emma asked.

The sheriff nodded. "Aggie told her exactly what to say. The hospital had no reason to question that the woman wasn't who she was supposed to be. As far as they knew, we sent them a homeless alcoholic named Aggie Wells. If she hadn't gone through alcohol withdrawal and almost died, it is hard to say how long it would have been before we discovered she wasn't Aggie Wells."

Emma shook her head. "You're afraid the real Aggie will come back here."

In the heavy silence that followed, Hoyt said, "If she isn't already here."

The sheriff looked uncomfortable. "I can't keep deputies watching the house."

"Of course you can't," Emma said, cutting off whatever her husband was about to say. "Nor can we live with a deputy parked outside our door."

"There's the chance that Aggie will run as far away as possible," the sheriff said. "I have been in touch with Aggie's brother and niece. They swear they haven't seen her, but I think the niece has. She's just a high school student, so I'm sure she had nothing to do with the switch with the homeless woman, but I think she gave her aunt money to get away. The brother definitely didn't help her. He promised to call if he heard anything from Aggie. I believe him."

"Someone helped her. I've worried all along that she has an accomplice," Hoyt said.

"Aggie made a lot of…maybe not friends, but people she helped over the years. She could have gotten any one of them to help her," the sheriff said. "Her brother said she used to brag about all the people who owed her and would do anything for her if she asked."

Hoyt swore under his breath.

"I'm following up on a lead concerning the driver of the mental hospital van who picked Aggie up in Whitehorse," the sheriff continued. "He was recently employed at the hospital. Apparently they go through a lot of staff. They had checked this driver's references and they were fine. But when they tried the numbers again, they'd been disconnected."

"Aggie really is incredible, isn't she," Emma said, awed by how Aggie had maneuvered her way out of this. She doubted there was anything the woman couldn't do if she set her mind to it. Including killing her. But if her original intent had been to frame Hoyt for the murder, she was going to have a much harder time doing it herself, given the trouble she was in.

"I just don't believe she wants to harm me," Emma said.

Hoyt scoffed at that. "She's crazy. Who knows what she'll do." He put a protective arm around his wife. "Find her," he said to the sheriff. "Find her before she strikes again. In the meantime, I'm not letting Emma out of my sight."

Emma groaned inwardly at the thought that she was now a prisoner in her own home.

AT THE BREAKFAST TABLE, Alexa studied her sister-in-law, torn between hoping it wasn't Sierra whom she'd seen with Jayden last night by the pond—and almost wishing it was. The sooner Landon got out of this house—and this marriage—the better off he'd be.

She hated that she felt this way and reminded herself that Landon adored Sierra. It would break his heart if his wife was cheating on him. But she couldn't help wondering if his "accidents" could have something to do with whatever Jayden was up to.

Alexa could feel even stronger undercurrents in this house this morning. Whatever had been at the edge of her consciousness gnawing to get in seemed even more determined as she excused herself and went to find her brother. She feared he needed more help than even he knew.

Sierra had said that she and Landon had taken a room on the north wing of the house, so she headed in that direction, hoping to talk to Landon alone. This house was such a maze of hallways that she quickly got turned around and wasn't even sure she was still headed north. She stopped to get her bearings and froze as she heard crying.

The desolate cry sounded like a woman sobbing her heart out. Goose bumps rippled across her flesh as she moved down the hall, the mournful wail growing louder, until the hallway ended. Stopping at the dead end, she stood listening. The crying seemed to be coming from inside the wall.

In this part of the house, a variety of woods had been used as a wainscoting that rose three-quarters of the way up each wall, with a very ornate, flocked wallpaper pattern on the upper part above it. Alexa touched the wood. It felt like a block of ice. She quickly drew back her fingers, unable to suppress a shudder.

Suddenly the crying stopped as quickly as it had begun. She took a step back and let out a startled yelp as she bumped into someone. Panicked, she spun around, half expecting to see the woman she'd heard crying.

"You heard her, didn't you?" Landon asked as he reached out to steady Alexa.

"Who?" Her heart was pounding. For

twenty-three years she'd avoided seeing dead people. Alexa didn't want that to change and yet, in this house, she feared that gnawing presence would win if she didn't get out of here soon.

Her brother gave her an impatient look. "The Crying Woman."

"The Crying Woman?" she repeated, trying to slow her racing pulse.

"That's what we all call her. We've all heard her at one time or another."

Her cynicism won out over her earlier fear. "But none of you have ever seen her, right?"

Landon swore. She could feel anger coming off him in waves and felt her own rise in her. His betrayal still stung. He'd gotten her here under false pretenses, and he'd told his wife and friends about her and their mother.

"How can you mock something you obviously heard as well?" he demanded furiously. "You do realize why you have to pretend it isn't real, don't you? It's like whistling in the dark. Well, sis, there's really something evil out there and you can whistle all you want, but that isn't going to save you. Or me."

She hated how much he sounded like their mother. "Could I have a word with you alone before you go down to breakfast?" She didn't like standing out here in this hallway. Not because she believed there was some crying woman ghost, but because she didn't want their conversation overheard. It was bad enough that the people in this house already knew their family secrets. She didn't want to add fuel to the fire.

He nodded, still clearly angry, but opened a door behind them and led her into the room he shared with Sierra. Like her own room, this one had been decorated with some of the same touches. Only this one had a fireplace, one that had been used recently. She caught the faint hint of smoke and saw that some papers had been burned. The lower corners of several sheets that hadn't fully burned could still be seen in the charred remains.

As she turned, she noticed her brother was limping. "What's wrong with your leg?"

He gave her an impatient look. "Another *accident*."

Her heart lodged in her throat and all her earlier resentment and anger toward him evaporated. "What happened?"

"I went down to get a glass of milk last night and I fell down the stairs." His tone made it clear that there was more to the story.

"Are you telling me someone pushed you?" she demanded.

"More like some*thing,* but what would be the point in telling *you?* You wouldn't believe me."

"Landon—"

"Alexa," he said, pleading suddenly in his voice, as well as fear. He stepped to her and took her shoulders in his hands. "You can exorcize whatever is wrong in this house. Mother used to—"

"It was a trick. Mother couldn't—"

He pulled free of her again, his face twisted in anguish. "You have always lied about your talents. Don't lie about Mother's. I saw her do amazing things time after—"

"It was all just illusion, Landon." Even as she said it, she knew it wasn't true. But she wished it was. If her mother had no gift, then her daughter couldn't have inherited it.

He stared at her in disbelief. "How can you discredit something that our mother believed in so strongly? It wasn't just what she did for a living." He moved to the window, turning his back to her as if he couldn't bear to look at her. "She wanted you to have what she did. She really did see it as a gift. While you…" He turned to face her again, his face twisted in pain. "You mock something I would give anything to have."

"Don't say that." She hurriedly crossed herself, the motion, like the words, coming before she could stop them.

His eyes narrowed. "You're afraid of it. That's why you block it. You think it's something evil."

"No, I told you—"

"Stop lying. You profess to be such a skeptic, a true cynic, but you just proved otherwise. What else are you lying about?"

"Landon—" Alexa reached for her brother, but he took a step back.

"I got you here because I desperately need your help. Don't even bother to tell me that you don't have the sight because I have *never* believed you. Maybe you fooled Mother—"

"Wouldn't that prove that she couldn't see as well as she pretended?"

He continued as if she hadn't spoken. "I know you, Alexa. You are the only person who can help me. Are you going to keep denying that you can't until it's too late?"

"Landon, I can see that something is wrong, but are you sure it isn't something more personal going on in this house?"

"Personal?" His face twisted into a mask

of pain. "You think this is about Sierra and me? You think she had something to do with my accidents?" He let out a choked laugh. "I know that you don't like her. That's it, isn't it? But that you'd think she would try to hurt me…"

"Landon—" Alexa reached for him again but he quickly sidestepped pass her and stormed out of the room.

She started to go after him but Sierra suddenly appeared in the doorway, blocking her exit.

MARSHALL FELT A LITTLE guilty for what he was doing. But he couldn't quit thinking about last night and Alexa Cross. She worried him a little. No, more than a little.

"Don't be looking at me like that," he said to his dog lying a few feet away. Angus sighed and closed his big, brown eyes as if to say, "Do whatever it is you have to do and leave me out of it."

"Oh, come on, you were as taken with her last night as I was," Marshall reminded the dog as he typed Alexa Cross into the computer and held his breath. Her name came up dozens of times. To his relief they were all pertaining to articles she'd written as a reporter for several newspapers during her career, including in Spokane, Washington, her latest job.

He felt relieved. She *was* a reporter, just as she'd said. Had he thought she'd lied about that? No. So what was bothering him?

Marshall laughed at the thought. A woman comes screaming across your pasture out of the darkness in the middle of the night dressed only in a thin—very thin—nightgown and faints in your arms. You have to wonder, right?

He moved the mouse down the list, taking note of the articles she'd written. Interesting, but nothing unusual or odd about any of them. In fact, the ones he called up and read were heartwarming stories about people. She had a nice writing style; he felt her compassion in the words she used.

She'd just had a bad dream last night, as he'd suspected.

His relief slipped away like fog as he recalled the first time he'd seen her. He could keep telling himself that it had just been a trick of the light. That there hadn't been anyone standing behind her. And if there had been, there was nothing…evil lurking there.

But he'd seen something that wasn't...of this earth.

And so had his horse. They'd both reacted to it. So how did he explain that away?

Marshall logged off the computer and checked his watch. He'd already wasted most of the morning, and he did have the cookies Emma had made to take to his new neighbors.

Grinning, he headed for the shower. Wouldn't hurt to take a day off. His father and brothers wouldn't miss him and it was only neighborly to stop over at the Wellington house and make sure Alexa was all right.

As he stepped under the warm spray of the shower, Marshall couldn't shake the feeling that Alexa was in some kind of trouble and that, more than a bad dream, it was what had sent her running across the pasture last night—as if running for her life.

SIERRA STEPPED INTO THE room, closed the door and leaned against it, making it clear that neither of them was going anywhere.

"What are you doing here?" she asked.

"Landon let me in—"

"Not this room. This house. Montana. What are you really doing here?" Sierra asked. "Did he tell you the house is haunted and you've come to exorcise our ghosts?"

"Don't be ridiculous. My brother—"

"Is it so ridiculous?" She raised an eyebrow. "I saw your reaction to the house. You might be able to fool Landon, but you can't fool me."

Alexa took a step toward her. "I'm not having this conversation with you again."

Sierra didn't move. "You shouldn't be here. Landon and I are technically still on our honeymoon."

Alexa almost laughed. "And that's why you invited five other people along?"

"They're friends."

Alexa felt her ire rise. "And I'm family."

"Yes, but it is clear that doesn't mean as much to you as it does to some," Sierra said. "I wouldn't say anything but you're upsetting Landon."

"He was upset before I got here. How many *accidents* has he had while in this house?"

Sierra rolled her eyes. "Who knew he was such a klutz, but then it is an old house and dangerous if you don't know what you're doing. Landon doesn't have much experience when it comes to handyman work."

As if the rest of this bunch were card-carrying finish carpenters.

"There isn't anyone here who might want to hurt him?" Alexa asked.

Sierra met her gaze with a steely-blue coldness that chilled Alexa to her soul. "I hope you didn't come here to cause trouble for me and your brother."

"I think there is already trouble enough in this house."

Her sister-in-law sighed. "I just came up to find you and inform you that breakfast is ready. You'd hate yourself if you missed out on Gigi's margarita pancakes." With that she turned and left the room.

Alexa stood for a moment, trying to still the apprehension she felt for her brother. He had no idea whom he'd married. But Alexa feared she did.

EMMA HAD BEEN GOING CRAZY ever since the sheriff had told them that Aggie Wells was missing. They didn't need to tell her that Aggie might be dangerous. The woman had abducted her only a few months ago.

But Emma couldn't live her life in fear, and she especially couldn't stand her husband hovering over her all the time. She knew Hoyt must be going crazy too. He needed to be out on the ranch working with his sons. It's what kept him young.

"Just let me go to the grocery store alone," she'd pleaded after the sheriff left; but, of course, he wasn't having any of it.

By the time they'd reached town, though, she knew she had to talk him into dropping her off at the grocery store while he ran his errands.

"It's the grocery store in broad daylight," she'd argued. "You don't really expect Aggie Wells to attack me in there, do you?"

"I don't know what she might do and neither do you," Hoyt said. "I told you I didn't want you out of my sight until she's caught."

"And what if she is never caught?"

He shook his head. "I just don't want anything to happen to you."

"I know," she said, touching his handsome face. "I appreciate your concern." What she didn't add, but wanted to, was that she couldn't keep living like this. This wasn't Hoyt's fault. Not unless you believed that he'd killed his other wives, which she didn't.

Even Aggie Wells, the former insurance investigator who'd been after him all these years, no longer believed Hoyt was a killer. Instead, she had another theory—one that had almost gotten her locked up in the mental hospital. Aggie was now convinced that Hoyt's first wife, Laura, had faked her accidental drowning and, being the jealous woman she apparently was, had become determined that Hoyt would never find happiness with another woman.

And that was why everyone thought Aggie was crazy. With the exception of Emma, who thought that was as good a theory as any.

The sheriff and Hoyt, though, believed Aggie was several bricks shy of a load and a dangerous, deranged murderer.

As Emma pushed through the doors into the town grocery, she shoved all thought of Aggie to the back burner and grabbed a cart. It just felt so good to be alone for a few minutes.

The town was small enough that she felt safe. She started in the produce aisle. The selection was pretty basic, but she loved fresh vegetables and began to load the cart. She nodded at other shoppers, spoke to a few and, after getting everything she needed plus some junk food she shouldn't have, she started through the checkout.

Suddenly she felt someone watching her.

As she looked out through the large plate-glass window at the front of the store, she felt a jolt of shock rocket through her.

Aggie Wells was standing across the street, staring right at her.

Her heart dropped—along with the half gallon of milk she was unloading from her cart—as her gaze locked with Aggie's.

A van went by, blocking her view. Her initial shock changed into anger. As long as Aggie was on the loose, Emma was going to be a prisoner in her own home and she was sick of it.

Stepping over the spilled milk, she ran out through the exit and into the parking lot. As she started across the street, she was almost struck by a pickup. The driver hit his brakes, missing her by inches, as she rushed across the street to where she'd seen the woman watching her.

Aggie was gone.

Emma stood, breathing hard, heart racing. She leaned over to catch her breath, hands on her knees, telling herself how foolish she'd been to chase after Aggie alone, when she saw the envelope lying at the edge of the sidewalk.

Written on it was one word: *Emma*.

Emma looked around, thinking Aggie couldn't have gone far. But there was no sign of her.

She picked up the envelope from the ground and stuffed it into her pocket as Hoyt drove up in the ranch pickup.

He gave her a surprised, questioning look that quickly turned to panic. Hoyt was out of the pickup in an instant and pulling her in his arms. Emma felt sick with guilt that she had resented this man's protection.

His gaze scanned the parking lot. "Where is she?"

Emma shook her head. He'd known the moment he saw her so there was no point in trying to lie her way out of it. "She got away."

He lowered his gaze to his wife and swore under his breath. "And the groceries?"

She glanced toward the store where a handful of people were gathered at the window, staring out at them.

"Everyone is going to think I've lost my mind," Emma said.

"They aren't the only ones," Hoyt said as he gripped her arm. "Let's go get our groceries."

ALEXA HAD NO INTEREST IN margarita pancakes, but she feared that if she didn't go down for breakfast, it could make things worse for her brother. She knew Sierra would use anything she could to put a wedge between her brother and her. The woman felt threatened. No doubt because Alexa saw through Sierra's act and she knew it.

She had worried for some time that part of Landon's allure had been the money their mother had left them. Remodeling this huge, old place was going to cost a fortune—even with free labor. Although Alexa hadn't seen much work getting done so far.

As she started to follow Sierra into the kitchen, she saw her brother seated at the kitchen table, his head down as he cut into his pancakes. He looked up as Sierra slid into a chair next to him and put her hand on his arm.

"Is everything all right?" he asked.

Sierra gave a little pout then looked over at Alexa.

Landon frowned as he followed her gaze, making it clear that he knew his sister had said something to hurt his wife's feelings.

Alexa felt her stomach roil as she saw how easy it was for Sierra to manipulate her brother. Love was definitely blind.

The loud doorbell startled everyone, including Alexa. Everyone looked toward the front door with a mixture of surprise and suspicion. Apparently they didn't get many visitors.

Since she was closest to the front door, she went to answer it. As the door swung open, she saw Marshall standing on the front step, looking up at the house and clearly giving it a mixed review. She felt herself smile, relieved to see him, and completely agreeing with his sentiments about the house that were written on his expressive face.

"Hello," she said, breathing in the morning air and his freshly showered scent.

He smiled. "Hello again." He removed his Stetson and handed her a small basket filled with what smelled like gingersnaps. "From my stepmother. A housewarming present." He turned the brim of the hat in his fingers, looking more than a little nervous. She liked his large hands, the strong, well-shaped fingers, the pads callused from hard ranch work.

She saw him look past her, peering into the house almost warily and yet with obvious curiosity. "I'd invite you in, but I was just on my way into town to pick up a few things." Not exactly true, but once said, she realized how badly she needed a break from this house and everyone in it. Also she knew Sierra would have a fit if she invited him in. And, even if she had wanted to share him, she had a pretty good idea of what the others' reaction would be to this cowboy.

Marshall brightened. "Great, how about lunch then?"

Her first instinct was to turn down his offer. She tended to keep people at a distance. It was easier that way. "Well, I do owe you after last night," she said, keeping her voice down so the others in the kitchen wouldn't hear.

He grinned. "I actually had a good time last night."

"Me too," she said, realizing that as strange as it was, it was true. "All right," she agreed. It was almost lunchtime and the last thing she wanted was margarita pancakes. "Why don't I follow you into town? Just give me a few minutes?"

As she glanced toward Marshall's pickup parked next to the house, she saw his dog sitting in the passenger seat and found herself smiling as she ran up to get her keys. There was nothing quite like a man and his dog.

"I'm having lunch in town," she said, sticking her head into the kitchen. She got the impression they'd all been holding their combined breaths, listening to every word anyway.

"You're missing margarita pancakes," Sierra said.

"My apologies to the chef," she said to Gigi, who obviously couldn't have cared less what Alexa had to eat.

But Sierra was pouting again. Alexa shot a look at her brother. How could Landon not notice his wife's obsessive need to control everyone around her?

Chapter Five

Alexa put her sister-in-law out of her mind as she drove through the rolling prairie, the morning sun warm, the sky a breathtaking blue. When she'd driven through Whitehorse yesterday, she hadn't been paying much attention. Landon had given her directions to Wellington Manor, and she'd been more worried about missing her turn than looking around the small town.

Now, though, as she drove in behind Marshall, she took in the small Montana town. It seemed a lot like others she'd driven through on her way here.

Situated around the railroad, the main drag faced the depot. She saw several bars, a clothing store, a hardware store, and a bank and electronics shop before she parked diagonally across from the depot and small town park.

"We had a fire last winter," Marshall said, when she asked about a newly graded area between two of the buildings. "Took out five businesses."

"That must have been a devastating blow to a town this size," she said.

"Fortunately, they all relocated into vacant buildings. Unfortunately, the population's dropping every year, like most small towns in this part of Montana," he said as he led her down the street to a restaurant. "But we also had a couple of new businesses start up this year, and some young couples are coming back because it's such a great place to raise a family."

Alexa smiled at his obvious love for this town. She could feel his close relationship with the land and this part of Montana. She liked that about Marshall Chisholm. She liked him.

The sign over the door of the restaurant read Northern Lights. He held the door for her and she stepped in, instantly assaulted by wonderful smells.

A young woman stuck her head out of the kitchen to tell them they could sit anywhere they liked.

"Thanks, Laci," Marshall said and explained on the way to their seat that Laci Duvall and her husband, Bridger, owned the restaurant and now had two young children. Her twin sister, Laney, also had two children pretty much the same ages and the rumor around town was that they were both pregnant again. "It must be a twin thing," he finished.

They walked over to a table by the window in time for Alexa to see a passenger train stop on the tracks just across the street in front of the small depot. By the time they'd sat down, the train had already loaded the half-dozen passengers waiting by the tracks and chugged off again.

"So how are you doing today?" Marshall asked.

"Better than I was last night. I apologize for waking you up and scaring you," she said.

"You looked more scared than I was."

She nodded and chewed at her lower lip for a moment. "I get nightmares sometimes, especially when I sleep in strange places."

"Nothing much stranger than that house your brother lives in."

She laughed. "You don't know the half of it."

A young waitress brought them menus and told them about the lunch special, which they quickly ordered: trout ravioli with the Northern Lights famous marinara sauce, salad and homemade garlic bread.

The owner sent out a carafe of red wine on the house, calling to Marshall to give his family her best and enjoy their lunch.

Alexa did. Both the food and company warmed her and she found herself opening up to this man she'd only just met. It wasn't like her. But last night had definitely made her drop her guard around him.

"You have *five* brothers?" She couldn't imagine what that must be like and said as much.

"It's just you and your brother?"

"He's my half brother. We have a mother in common." She looked away, hoping he didn't ask about their mother.

"All six of us are adopted, three of us having the same mother and father," he said. "My mother was Norwegian, my father Assiniboine. Three of my brothers are triplets. They're blond and blue-eyed. We make quite the family."

She loved hearing what it was like growing up in a large ranch family. "It must be wonderful."

He laughed at that. "You haven't seen the

way we fight. But let anyone else pick on one of us and he'll have all six to contend with."

At his prompting, she told him about her job at the newspaper. "I love interviewing people, writing their stories. Mostly I do feature writing, no hard news." She liked upbeat stories and was glad to let someone else write about fires and crime and misery. "Don't laugh, but I've always wanted to write children's books."

"I'm in awe," Marshall said. "I hate to write a check."

They both laughed and he asked, "So where did you grow up?"

"California." Fortunately the waitress brought them Laci's famous flourless chocolate cake for dessert and Alexa was able to change the subject. "I haven't eaten this much ever," she said as she took another bite of the cake. "It was all so delicious."

"Laci will be glad to hear it. Where in California?"

"The Laguna Beach area. So tell me about the Chisholm Cattle Company," she said, steering the conversation away from her once again.

But she had the feeling that Marshall wasn't fooled. Nor had she curbed his curiosity. His interest in her both flattered her and scared her. She had learned the hard way that once men found out who her mother had been, they suddenly felt uneasy around her and didn't call again.

She liked Marshall, but she was only here for a few days and she had her hands full back at the house. She warned herself not to get too close. Or worse, let him.

"I really need to get back to the house," she said at the thought of the trouble her brother was in.

Marshall looked disappointed, but quickly asked for the check. "Maybe we'll see each other again. I'll pick up more beer at the store in case you have another bad dream. Or just want to talk some night."

Alexa felt the pull of this man and quickly thanked him for lunch. "Please thank your stepmother as well for the cookies." As they left the restaurant, she told herself she wouldn't see Marshall Chisholm again before she left town, and it was probably just as well.

She recalled her first impression. Desire and darkness. While she felt drawn to him, she didn't want him getting involved in whatever was going on at Wellington Manor. The desire she felt scared her. But the darkness terrified her. She feared it was because he had crossed her path.

As he tipped his Stetson, climbed into his truck next to Angus and pulled away, she couldn't help feeling a sense of regret.

MARSHALL GLANCED BACK in his pickup's rear-view mirror. Alexa Cross was still standing next to her car, watching him drive away. Something in her expression reminded him of the first time he'd seen her standing at the window—and whatever that had been behind her.

He also recalled the way she hadn't invited him in this morning. That hadn't been like her. Just as she had seemed to want to get away from that house as quickly as possible.

"Something's wrong over there," he said to Angus, who'd curled up on the seat for his usual nap on the ride home.

He didn't like the idea of Alexa staying at that house, but he reminded himself that it wasn't any of his business. He had cattle to help move today and a list a mile long of things to do at his house later, and yet his thoughts kept returning to her.

"What do you even know about this woman?" his brother Tanner asked as they moved cattle that afternoon. It was one of those amazing August afternoons when the sky is a crystalline blue stretched from horizon to horizon, with only a few white clouds moving in the breeze.

The sun felt hot against his back as they rode across the same rolling prairie that thousands of buffalo had once roamed. Marshall took off his hat to mop his brow with his sleeve. What *did* he know about Alexa Cross?

"She's a newspaper reporter, won some awards for her writing, has a half brother who's married to a Wellington." That was the extent of what he knew—at least on the surface.

He also knew her laugh, knew the way she felt in his arms, knew that she was up for a beer at sunrise and that something had her running scared.

"I like her," he said defensively.

Tanner laughed. "I gathered that since she's all you've talked about this entire cattle drive." He shook his head. "I never thought I'd see the day you'd get hung up on a city woman, let alone a *reporter.*"

"She wants to write children's books," he called after Tanner, as his brother spurred his horse and took off in a cloud of dust after a couple of straggling calves.

Marshall sat back on his horse, watching the undulating ocean of Black Angus cattle moving across the prairie. Tanner thought he had fallen for this woman? Marshall laughed at the thought, then sobered as he realized he'd never felt this way about any other woman—or so quickly. Both thoughts sent up red flags.

He'd dated, like his brothers, sowing his wild oats but never getting serious about anyone. Then one by one, his brothers were starting to fall in love. He was a little insulted that Tanner had thought he would never see the day that Marshall fell in love.

"All it takes is meeting the right person," Emma had said once about how she and Hoyt had fallen in love. "You know immediately."

Marshall heard a shrill whistle, saw his brother Dawson pointing to some calves that had fallen behind. He spurred his horse to ride after them, embarrassed that he'd been sitting on his horse woolgathering instead of working. He'd get a ribbing about it later.

But as he thought about Alexa Cross, he knew he had worse problems than a little ribbing from his brothers.

ALEXA FELT BETTER AFTER her lunch with Marshall. He was so down-to-earth, so…normal. She smiled at the thought. She'd aspired to be normal, or what she had thought of as a child as normal. She really hadn't had much to base it on—other than her father.

He had been so normal, though, he hadn't been able to take living with Tallulah and her "gift" any longer. Is that another reason Alexa hadn't wanted to be like her mother? And why she kept her past life secret? Because she doubted any man could live with a woman like that.

As she drove up the tree-lined lane that led to Wellington Manor, she felt her earlier calm evaporate.

There was an ambulance parked in front of the house.

She pulled her SUV up next to it and hurried toward the front door as an EMT was coming out. "What's happened?" she cried, thinking of her brother and his recent series of accidents.

"Just a minor concussion," the EMT said as he loaded his gear into the back of the ambulance. "He's going to be fine."

A minor concussion? Alexa ran into the house, crying her brother's name. She came to an abrupt stop as Landon stepped out of the kitchen with half of a sandwich in his hand and a frown on his handsome face.

"Why are you screaming for me?" he demanded.

"I thought…" The rest of her words died in her throat. She took a shaky breath as she saw several of the others looking at her as if she'd lost her mind. "I saw the ambulance."

Her brother seemed to realize exactly what she'd thought, and said, "Jayden. A pipe fell in the basement. He has a slight concussion. He'd just come over to help me when it happened."

She had the feeling he was enjoying her fear, now that he realized it had been for him. But his look also said, "It could have been me, no thanks to you."

"So you're still working on that leak in the basement?" she asked because she couldn't think of anything else to say.

"Upstairs bedroom. I got it fixed," Landon said and turned back to the kitchen where everyone had been having a late lunch.

She wondered how they ever got anything done as she tried to still her racing pulse. She'd been so sure the ambulance had been here for her brother. As she let out a breath, she felt guilty for her relief that it hadn't been Landon.

"Is Jayden all right?" she asked.

"He'll live," Archer said with apparently little interest. He was reading a book and eating a sandwich and didn't bother to look up.

As she glanced around those sitting at the table, Alexa saw that along with Jayden, the only other person missing was Sierra. She started to ask about her but her brother cut her off.

"Sierra took the first shift to make sure Jayden doesn't fall asleep," Landon said. "So how was *your* lunch?"

"Good." No one at the table seemed in the least bit curious but she continued, "Marshall took me to Northern Lights. The owner makes the best ravioli I've ever had."

"Marshall Chisholm?" Gigi asked, looking up. "Sierra said he had a house on the other side of the pond. So he's a real cowboy?" she added with a smirk.

"His family ranches. The Chisholm Cattle Company," Alexa said, wanting to defend Marshall but also not wanting to be baited into it.

"That's a big operation," Devlin said with

awe. "I heard in town it's the largest working cattle ranch around here. So was your date the owner?"

"One of six sons."

He looked disappointed for her as if she'd missed a real opportunity. Gigi wasn't smirking anymore, at least.

"I need to get back to work," Landon said as he finished his sandwich.

"Oh, I was hoping we could visit for a moment," Alexa said as he started past her.

"Archer and I promised Sierra we would have the bathroom done before supper," he said as Archer got to his feet as well. "Find something to amuse yourself. We can visit later."

"Don't forget," Gigi spoke up. "Sierra said she had something fun planned for tonight after supper."

Alexa had to bite her tongue not to groan. "Why don't you come up to my room when you get done with your jobs. Maybe we can talk before supper," she said to her brother.

She could tell he was still angry with her. Unreasonably, she thought with irritation. But then another person had been hurt in this house. Jayden this time. She wondered though if the *accident* had been meant for Landon. Or if that was all it had been, an accident.

As she watched her brother head off down the hall toward the servants' quarters, where his wife was telling stories to Jayden to keep him awake, she knew he'd gone to check on Sierra before going upstairs to work in the bathroom.

How could she make him see what she suspected was going on in this house? She realized there was only one way.

As she started up the stairs, she saw a bucket of tools someone had left in the corner. Taking a few items she didn't think would be missed, including a flashlight, she hurried up the steps to the second floor.

Alexa suspected that someone in this house wanted everyone to believe Wellington Manor was haunted. For what reason, she had no idea yet. But for now, it was time to expose the Crying Woman for the fake she was. At least it would be a start in exposing whatever else was going on inside Wellington Manor.

EMMA FELT BADLY ABOUT not telling Hoyt everything after how scared he'd been at the grocery store. But she told herself she didn't want to upset him further. He'd hardly said a word all the way home, and she could tell he was stewing in a brew of anger and fear, all of it directed at Aggie Wells.

When they reached the ranch house, he said, "Stay here. Keep the doors locked. I want to check the house."

Emma started to argue but one look at his expression warned her to keep her mouth shut.

She watched him take the shotgun from behind the seat in the pickup, close the truck door and stand outside until he heard her lock the cab, before he walked toward the house.

Emma waited until he went inside before she pulled the envelope from her pocket. Her fingers were trembling.

All the way home from Whitehorse, she'd been going over what had happened and what it all meant. Aggie was still in town. She'd taken a huge chance showing herself the way she had. What if Hoyt had been in the parking lot and seen her?

Had Aggie followed them from the ranch? How else would she know where they were going? With a start, Emma realized that she had become a creature of habit, shopping every Wednesday after lunch when the ads came out in the newspaper.

Emma recalled what Aggie had told her about why she'd been such a good insurance investigator. "I become my subjects. I learn everything about them. I dress like them, listen to the same music, wear the same perfume."

That was why Aggie had known Emma would run out of the grocery store after her. That frightened Emma more than anything else, because there was a good chance she was dealing with a murderer who knew her too well.

Emma carefully opened the envelope and took out the single sheet of paper. Had Aggie planned to hand this to her? Or had she always planned to leave it on the sidewalk?

Not that it much mattered. Aggie had taken a huge risk getting it to her. That alone showed an unsettling desperation. This woman was a wanted, escaped criminal who just wouldn't give up in her quest.

And that quest apparently was either to save Emma or kill her. No one knew for sure which it was, Emma included.

She unfolded the page of plain white paper.

Emma,
I've found Laura Chisholm. I can prove

*it. We have to talk. But if you go to the
sheriff or do anything that will alert
Laura, it will mean your life.*
Aggie

Under her name she had written what
Emma recognized as a local cell phone
number.

The front door of the house opened. Emma
hurriedly refolded the paper and stuffed it and
the envelope into her jacket pocket as Hoyt
returned to the pickup.

"The house is empty," he said as he put his
shotgun back up on the rack behind the seat.
"Are you all right?"

Telling herself she just wasn't ready to talk
to him about this, she said, "I guess it is just
starting to sink in."

He nodded, looking relieved. "The woman
is crazy and dangerous and I wish I didn't
have to keep telling you that."

Emma nodded as she got out of the pickup.
She wished she wasn't so stubborn and independent and hard to get along with too.

"She thinks my first wife is still alive," Hoyt
said as if Emma didn't know that as well.

"What if she is?" Emma said and instantly
regretted it when his face clouded over.

"I saw Laura go into the water," Hoyt said, pain making his voice sound hoarse. "She hated water, didn't know how to swim well and with the storm and the waves..." His voice broke. "I saw her go under, Emma. I almost drowned trying to save her. There is no way she could have swum to shore from the middle of the Fort Peck Reservoir...." He ran out of words again and gave her an impatient look before stalking into the house.

Emma told herself he was right, of course. But she reached into her pocket to make sure the note was still there. But she couldn't help thinking about what Aggie had written. She had *proof* Laura was alive. What if it was true? What if Aggie wasn't the killer at all? What if it really was Hoyt's first wife back from the grave?

What scared Emma was that while Hoyt was trying to protect her from Aggie Wells, there could be someone more dangerous out there who wanted her dead—and none of them would see Laura Chisholm coming.

ALEXA RAN HER FINGERS along the expensive wood of the wainscoting, starting from the place where she'd first heard the Crying

Woman and moving down the hall to where it ended—and the crying had stopped.

She told herself that someone must have activated the crying with some sort of device this morning after she'd said she was going upstairs to see her brother, because she heard nothing now. But then no one knew she was up here.

But who had turned it off? Or was it on a timer? Either way, someone in this house had set up the device. Not hard to believe, given this new generation that was raised with computers and all the other high-tech toys.

But why would anyone go to the trouble? Why make her and the rest of the people in this house believe it was haunted? She feared the reason had something to do with Landon. He believed the house was trying to either scare him away—or kill him.

Alexa knew someone in this house wanted him to leave. Sierra? That made no sense, since she was the one who was pushing to remodel the house and run it as a bed-and-breakfast. Unless she'd decided the marriage wasn't going to work out and she knew about Landon's inheritance. Their mother had left them a lot of money. Knowing her brother, he'd probably told Sierra about it long before their nuptials.

Alexa moved quietly down the wall, feeling her way along. She wasn't even sure what exactly she was looking for. There didn't seem to be anything along the wall. Nor were there any doors on this side of the hall other than one at the very end. She tried the door. Of course it was locked. Why have a locked room?

She was about to find out. Using the screwdriver, she was able to open the old skeleton-key lock. The door swung in as if on a gust of wind. The room appeared to be a broom closet—at least at first.

Alexa stepped in and, turning on the flashlight, searched for a secret door. She found the panel in the wall easily enough, since she knew it had to be there. It swung in. Musty air wafted out.

As she shone the flashlight into the dark, dusty space, she found a long, narrow aisle that ran adjacent to the hallway outside this room. What surprised her were two sets of stairs—one that went up to the third floor, the other down to the ground floor and a door outside. A secret passage—and another way out of the house.

Sierra hadn't taken her up to the third floor during her tour. She'd made the excuse that it was unfinished and full of spider webs and storage items. Alexa would have loved to see for herself, but she had to find the Crying Woman first.

At a sound from the hallway, she froze, listening. When she didn't hear anything more, she shone the flashlight down the narrow aisle behind the stairway. No spider webs, but footprints in the dust. She wasn't the first person to squeeze through the opening and into the space behind the wall.

Alexa hadn't gone far when she found the wires and small speakers. She was looking for what was being used to operate the Crying Woman, when she heard the same sound from the hallway she'd heard earlier.

Only this time, she realized it wasn't coming from beyond the wall. It was from a person in the space with her.

She swung around with the flashlight, but too late. The blow knocked her into the wall. She smacked her head hard, stars dancing in her vision as the flashlight fell from her hand, hitting the floor with a thud just an instant before Alexa joined it.

Chapter Six

Alexa woke in her bed to find everyone standing around her. Her brother was holding her hand and looking scared.

"I'm going to have to insist you not explore this house alone again," Sierra said, her voice shrill. "You could have been killed. If Archer hadn't found you…" She looked as if she was going to cry.

Landon put his arm around his wife but still held tight to Alexa's hand. "Alexa's all right," he said, trying to reassure his wife, but he looked at his sister for confirmation.

"I'm fine," she said, although her head ached and for a few moments, she couldn't remember what had happened. As it came back, she said, "Archer found me?"

The big man nodded. "I was coming down the hall when I saw you lying on the floor at the end of it."

"You found me out in the hallway?" she

asked, knowing that couldn't be true. The last thing she remembered was that she had been behind the wall.

"I can't imagine what you were doing in the north wing to begin with," Sierra said.

"I'm sure she probably just got turned around. Are you sure you're all right?" Landon asked again as he saw her check her clothing.

Just as she'd thought, she was covered in dust. As she looked up, she saw all of them watching her. One of them had carried her out of that space behind the wall and left her in the hallway to be found. She wanted desperately to ask Archer how it was he had just happened along when he did. Either he was lying or someone had sent him up to that hallway knowing he would find her.

"I'm just a little tired," Alexa said, not wanting to question Archer in front of the rest of them.

"You're sure she doesn't have a concussion?" Sierra asked her husband.

But it was Jayden who answered. "I checked her pupils. They seem fine. Nothing like mine yesterday."

"Remodeling this house ourselves was a mistake," Sierra cried. "I can't bear to see anyone else get hurt. Landon, I should have listened to you. It's too dangerous."

"Don't you dare back out now," Carolina said. "Everyone is fine and this is *our* project. We've done too much work for you to make us stop now."

"She's right," Jayden said. "We're all invested in this old place. Let us finish."

Alexa saw Sierra weaken and suspected she hadn't been serious to begin with. "If I hired contractors, they would kick us all out until it was finished," she said. "And we do love that our closest friends are a part of our adventure."

Landon looked as if he wanted to object, but it was already decided. Everyone started to leave the room to go back to work. Her brother let go of her hand to follow them out.

"Landon, can you please stay for a moment?" Alexa asked.

He hesitated. Sierra had turned at the door waiting for him. "I'll be down in just a moment," he told her.

Sierra shifted her gaze to Alexa, anger flashing in her eyes, then she smiled a weak smile. "Make her promise she won't be wandering around the house anymore," she said and left.

"Close the door," Alexa said quietly to her brother.

He studied her a moment before walking over and closing the door. "Want to tell me what really happened to you? Or are you still in denial about this house and the spirits in it?"

She didn't want to fight with him, even if she'd had the energy. "I found your Crying Woman," she said as she swung her legs over the edge of the bed and started to stand.

He moved quickly to grab her arm as she suddenly felt lightheaded and had to sit back down on the edge of the bed for a moment.

"What are you doing? You need to rest."

"No, I need to show you something." She moved to the door, opened it and looked out, half expecting to find Sierra or one of the others lurking there. The hallway was empty. "Come on," she said to her brother as she pulled the old skeleton key from her door and headed down the hall.

As he followed her to the north wing of the house, she motioned to him to be quiet. He rolled his eyes, but didn't argue.

Once at the broom closet door, she used the key to get inside. The panel slid back just as it had earlier. As she started to step through the opening, Landon grabbed her arm.

"You shouldn't go in there," he said. "Sierra doesn't want—"

"Inside here is where someone hit me and knocked me out," Alexa said. "I didn't faint out in the hallway and hit my head. Look at the dust on my clothes."

He released her and she stepped through, squeezed through the narrow space between the stairs and hallway wall and stopped at the spot where she'd found the speakers.

It took a moment for her eyes to adjust to the darkness. She could hear Landon next to her.

"What are we doing?" he asked.

She wished she'd thought to have him bring a flashlight, but she hadn't wanted the others knowing what they were up to. "Strike a match." She suspected he still had matches from the fire he'd built for Sierra in their room.

In the blackness, she could hear him rummaging in his pocket. A moment later came the scratch of the match head. She'd been right and was now all the more curious about the papers Sierra had burned.

The small burst of the light illuminated the

interior wall. Alexa stared at the wall, telling herself she shouldn't have been surprised. The wiring and speakers were gone. Whoever had struck her had taken her proof.

She looked over at her brother as the match burned down. "It's gone. The wiring, the speakers, the Crying Woman deception. I didn't get a chance to find the rest of the device before I was struck by whoever was in here with me."

Just before the flame died, Alexa saw her brother's expression. He thought she was lying. Again.

MARSHALL WAS RELIEVED WHEN he got Alexa on the phone. "Are you all right? When I stopped by earlier, the woman who answered the door said you'd had an accident and couldn't come down."

"Was the woman blonde, bossy and seemed to be put out that she'd had to answer the door?" Alexa asked.

He let out a laugh, relieved that she sounded fine. "As a matter of fact, she was."

"That's Sierra Wellington Cross, my sister-in-law."

"So you're all right?"

"None the worse for wear."

Something in her voice told him she wasn't as fine as she was pretending to be. Her scream as she'd run across his pasture last night was too fresh in his mind. He couldn't shake the feeling that there was more to her bad dream than she was letting on. And now she'd had an accident? He was all the more anxious about her staying in that house.

"Have supper with me," he said impulsively.

"My sister-in-law has something planned for this evening. Can I take a rain check?" She forgot she wasn't going to see him again.

"Sure. Why don't you give me a call when you can get away," Marshall said and gave her his number. "Call any time. Even in the middle of the night if you have another bad dream."

She chuckled. "You don't mean that."

"I do. The truth is I'm worried about you being in that house, especially after I heard that you fainted and hit your head. That is what happened, isn't it?"

He heard a click on the line.

"I appreciate your concern," Alexa said. "We'll talk soon."

As he hung up, Marshall knew why her voice had changed and she'd quickly gotten off the line. Someone had picked up another line in the house and was listening in.

ALEXA HAD HEARD THE CLICK as well. She'd heard the person on the line, felt them listening to her conversation. Sierra?

After returning to her bed on Landon's orders, she'd waited until she was sure he'd gone back downstairs with the others before she'd taken her key again and gone over to the north wing.

She'd tapped lightly at Sierra and Landon's bedroom door, then had let herself in, feeling like a thief in the night. But she had to know what Sierra had burned in the fireplace. It was probably nothing, and yet she had the feeling that Sierra didn't do anything without a good reason.

Burning papers instead of just throwing them away made Alexa suspicious. Using the poker, she carefully dug the unburned portions out of the ashes, shook them off and gave them a cursory glance before hightailing it back to her room.

Once there, she tried to make sense of what appeared to be financial documents. She couldn't and found herself wondering if she hadn't wasted her time retrieving them.

There were a couple of names she could make out. She started to write them down when a tap at the door made her jump.

Sierra stuck her head in. "Supper's ready. Gigi cooked her famous chicken enchiladas. I hope you feel well enough to come down. You already missed her margarita pancakes. You can't miss the enchiladas."

Her stomach growled in answer as she covered the partially burned documents with a book she'd been reading. "I wouldn't dream of it."

"You do feel up to coming down, don't you? We're going to play charades after dinner in the main hall. Your brother is terrible at it so I want you on our team. Hurry down. Everyone is waiting," she said and closed the door.

Alexa groaned as she hurriedly wrote the two names from the document into her notebook that she always carried for reporting at the newspaper, put it back in her purse and picked up her wrap from the chair where she'd thrown it earlier. This drafty old house was starting to get to her, but she couldn't let on. They were all watching her, probably more closely than ever after today's incident.

On her way down the hall, she noticed the phone in a small alcove. It could have been

Sierra who picked up the line and listened in. Alexa wouldn't have put it past her.

Hurrying down to the kitchen, she found Gigi making margaritas to go with dinner. Everyone seemed in great spirits. Except Landon. He didn't look up as Alexa took her place at the table amid all the lively conversation and laughter.

After they'd left the space behind the wall earlier, he'd accused her of making up what she'd seen rather than accepting that the Crying Woman was one of many spirits trapped in this house.

"If I can feel something in this house, then you sure as hell can," he'd said. "Do you want to know what Mother told me on her deathbed?"

She hadn't. Not that she could have stopped him, though, from telling her.

"She said if I ever needed you, you would quit lying about your gift and help me. Don't you see? She had seen the future. She knew about this place."

That was such a leap that Alexa had only stared at him speechless. "I am trying to help you," she said finally.

"Are you?"

She had silently cursed her mother for

this as she'd watched her brother walk away. Landon would rather believe in the paranormal than what was right in front of him. Someone in this house was behind all of this and as Alexa accepted a margarita, she felt even more determined to find out who it could be.

She'd proven, at least to herself, that someone was behind the Crying Woman. But her brother was right. There were other things in this house. She needed to learn the history of this house and the people who had lived in it, because she suspected whoever was behind the Crying Woman already had.

Alexa couldn't wait to talk to Marshall. She was sure he would know the history of Wellington Manor or who to talk to about it. But there was no way she could get out of dinner or charades. She took a sip of her margarita. It tasted wonderful and it numbed her senses just enough that she didn't feel the house watching her—as well as the people in it.

HOYT HAD CALLED THE sheriff the moment he'd entered the ranch house.

"You're sure it was Aggie?" was McCall's

first question when she arrived twenty minutes later.

"It was her." Emma knew she could prove it by producing the note, but she wasn't ready to do that and it wasn't as if by having the note, the sheriff could find Aggie.

She knew it was crazy, but Aggie was trusting her and she couldn't betray that trust. Had she said that to Hoyt he would have had her head examined.

Everyone believed that Aggie wanted her dead. But Aggie'd had all kinds of chances to kill her when she'd abducted her—and hadn't. Aggie swore she was trying to save her and a part of Emma believed her.

The trouble was that no one believed Laura Chisholm was still alive. Even Emma, but especially Hoyt. But what if Laura was? Hoyt had admitted that Laura was horribly jealous in the short period of time they were married before she was believed to have drowned.

"Did she say something to you?" the sheriff asked Emma.

"No. By the time I ran out of the store and across the street she was gone."

McCall frowned. "Why did you run after her?"

"That's what I'd like to know," Hoyt said.

Emma could tell he was scared and that made him all the more angry with her for taking a chance like that. "What if Aggie had had a gun?"

"I just saw her standing there and didn't think," Emma said. "She looked as if she wanted to say something to me."

"And yet she disappeared when you came out of the store?" the sheriff said.

Emma nodded. "I think she was scared off."

"I hope she was scared out of town," Hoyt said.

The sheriff shook her head. "I doubt that's the case. I'm surprised she would take such a chance to see you—or have you see her. That was reckless on her part."

Hoyt shot his wife a look. "That's what frightens me. You would think she'd have the good sense to skip the country. Who knows what the woman will do next?"

After the sheriff left, Hoyt finally went out to feed the horses and left Emma alone for a few moments, something that surprised her.

She was just about to make the call to Aggie when the back door opened and two of her stepsons came in. Emma realized that

Hoyt had called them to watch over her until he got back from the barn.

After visiting for a few minutes, she excused herself and went upstairs to her bathroom. Closing the door, she pulled out her cell phone and the note from Aggie.

Reading it again, she debated what she was about to do. She did tend to be impulsive. But she'd learned as she'd gotten older to follow her own instincts.

She dialed the number and listened as the phone began to ring.

EVERYONE WAS A LITTLE tipsy by the time they'd played charades. Alexa enjoyed herself even though Sierra was disappointed her team didn't win.

"Sorry, I'm terrible at charades," she told her sister-in-law later that evening.

Sierra gave her a look that said she hadn't been trying or, even worse, had been cheating. The woman really didn't understand how Alexa's "powers" worked.

Everyone but Carolina and Alexa got up and wandered into the kitchen for a midnight snack. Carolina had been quiet all evening, seemingly lost in her own thoughts.

Now she moved over to sit next to Alexa on

the couch. "Please," she said sounding close to tears. "Tell me my future." She held out her hand, palm up.

"I'm sorry, I don't—"

"Please." There was pleading in her gaze. "I have to *know.*"

"Palm reading is just a parlor game," Alexa said, not unkindly, but she took the woman's hand, unable to ignore the pain she saw in her eyes. As she idly ran her thumb across Carolina's palm, she had planned to tell her that she saw a rosy future, but the words caught in her throat as she felt a jolt race up her arm.

She let go of Carolina's hand as if it were a deadly snake.

"What?" the young woman cried.

Alexa felt the weight of what she'd seen pressing against her chest. "It's nothing. Just a cramp in my fingers."

Carolina stared down at her palm. "It's bad, isn't it? I knew it was bad."

"I told you palm reading is nothing more than a parlor game," Alexa said, trying to reassure her. "No one can tell your future by looking at your palm."

She was angry with herself for not only scaring the woman, but also scaring herself. She realized the margaritas had weakened the barriers she'd built up and, while she'd sensed horror and dread, she couldn't have told Carolina what would happen in her future or when—only that it would be very bad.

"You are going to have everything you want out of life," she said, the lie almost choking her.

Carolina looked a little less stricken. "Really?"

"Absolutely." Alexa remembered what her mother had said when Landon had once asked, "What do you do when you are looking into a client's future and you see something bad?"

"I look for something good. I never lie," Tallulah Cross had said. "The last thing you want to do is lie." She had looked over at Alexa then, the warning clear.

"What will happen if you do lie?" Alexa had asked. She must have been all of ten years old at the time. Her brother a precocious five.

"You don't want to know," her mother had said.

Alexa had just lied. But then she'd been lying for twenty-three years, hadn't she?

AGGIE WELLS ANSWERED ON the fourth ring. Emma had been about to hang up when Aggie picked up. She sounded so…normal, not at all like a delusional criminal who had law enforcement officers across the country looking for her.

"I'm glad you called," Aggie said. "I've been so worried about you."

"Aggie, you need to turn yourself in so you can—"

"Get locked up in the state mental hospital? Emma, you wouldn't have called me if you thought I was crazy."

Emma sighed. "How could Laura Chisholm be alive?"

"I don't know. I just know that she is and I can prove it. I have photographs of the woman."

"Why haven't you taken the information to the sheriff?" Emma asked.

"I can't trust that Laura won't find out and get away again. She's been like a chameleon since she allegedly died thirty years ago. That's why she's been so hard to track down."

Did Emma really believe any of this? "You found her?"

"She was only a few hours away from Whitehorse. She will be coming after you next, Emma."

Emma could well imagine what Hoyt or

the sheriff might say about this. "How can you be sure she's Laura?"

"She's changed over the years, of course. Some of the changes I'm sure were so no one in Whitehorse would recognize her, but I have no doubt that Hoyt will be able to."

"You said you had proof," Emma said, thinking that even if the woman was Hoyt's first wife, it wouldn't prove that she killed his other wives or that she was after his fourth—her.

"Meet me and I will give you the photographs and all the information about Laura."

"Why don't you send it to me?"

"You know why. Hoyt might intercept it and call in the sheriff," Aggie said. "If Laura is scared away, she might not surface for a long time. Neither of us will ever be safe until she is caught."

"I don't understand how my getting the information—"

"Come on, Emma, of course you do. You and I have to trap her. She wants you. She's biding her time and will strike when you least expect it. But if we go after her—"

"You want to use me as bait?"

"Don't sound so shocked. I've come to know you, Emma. You're tough as nails. I'd want you on my side in any fight. I hope you realize that I'm good at what I do and I'm not some crazy woman. Obsessed, maybe. I want to solve this. If I get sent back to the state mental hospital, Laura will kill you and who knows what they'll do with me. I have to see this through. You can understand that, can't you?"

Emma thought of her ex and the chance she'd taken to make sure the bastard went to prison for what he'd done. She also thought about her life right now and Hoyt's. This had to end. Even if it only ended with Aggie being caught—and some woman who might look like Laura Chisholm being cleared.

"When?" she asked.

"You're going to have to come up with some way to get Hoyt off your tail, so to speak. You think you can do that tomorrow?"

"It won't be easy getting away from Hoyt," Emma said. "He wouldn't let me go into town by myself before I saw you. Now he will insist on going into the store with me."

"That's why I think we should meet on the ranch," Aggie said.

"How would you suggest we do that?"

"There is a trail behind the house that goes down to the river. It's not that far. All you have to do is figure out a way to get out of his sight for a few minutes. Once you're in the trees, he won't know where you've gone."

"And when I come back up from the river?" Emma asked.

"I'm afraid you are going to have to lie about where you've been and why."

"I don't like doing that." Especially when Hoyt was just trying to keep her safe.

"You haven't told him about the note I left you—or this call, have you," Aggie said. "You're doing this for him as well as for yourself."

Emma couldn't argue that. She still questioned why they had to meet in person and said as much.

"I have to know I can trust you," Aggie said. "Once you see the evidence I have, we'll take the next step."

The next step being the two of them taking this woman down? Emma knew she was taking a hell of a chance just meeting Aggie.

But, while she couldn't tell Hoyt or the sheriff this, she believed Aggie was trying to help her. She thought if she met with Aggie, she could convince her to turn herself in.

"Tomorrow afternoon," Aggie said. "Try

to come after lunch. I know Hoyt likes to go out and check his horses after lunch."

Yes, Aggie knew a lot about them. The insurance company she used to work for said Aggie was the best investigator they'd ever had.

So wasn't it possible she could be right about Laura Chisholm being alive?

"I'll wait for you until two-thirty," Aggie said and hung up.

When Emma came out of the bathroom, Hoyt was waiting for her.

Chapter Seven

Marshall looked up in surprise at the knock on his front door. He hadn't heard a vehicle nor was he expecting anyone this late.

When he opened the door he was even more surprised. "Not another bad dream, I hope," he said as he motioned Alexa in.

"I know it's late, but you still had a light on...."

"I couldn't sleep," he said as she stepped in. "How about you?" he asked, studying her. She was beautiful, so exotic and apparently wide-awake this time. But he still sensed a desperation in her like she'd had the first time she'd come to visit late at night.

"Couldn't sleep," she said, appearing uncomfortable. He guessed her showing up here had been impulsive and was something she was now regretting.

"Sit down. I'll get us a beer. I bought extra,

hoping you'd stop by," he said and started toward the kitchen.

"None for me, thanks. But I would take a glass of water."

He returned a few moments later, not sure she would still be there. She was. He felt relieved even though she was still standing. She took the glass of water he offered her and finally sat down.

"Are you all right after your fall?" he asked.

"Marshall..."

It was the first time she'd used his name. He liked the way she said it and found himself looking at her bow-shaped lips. Just the thought of kissing her—

"Can I be honest with you?"

"Do you really even have to ask?" he said as he dropped into the chair across from her.

"My brother thinks Wellington Manor is haunted," she said.

"What makes you think it isn't?" He could see she was surprised by his response.

"I'm sorry, but you don't seem like a man who believes in ghosts," she said.

He smiled at that. "Since we're being honest, the first time I saw you, you could have made me a believer. I thought you were a ghost and—" He shook his head. "I still wasn't sure when I saw you come running across my pasture."

ALEXA HAD GLIMPSED SOMETHING cross Marshall's features and remembered the first time she'd seen *him*—and that odd sense of desire and darkness she'd felt.

"What was it you were going to say a moment ago, but changed your mind?" she asked.

He was taken aback by the question.

"I'm sorry but I saw the change in your expression. Was it something about the first time you saw me?"

Marshall studied her for a moment. "Not much misses your attention, does it?"

"I told you. I'm a reporter. You have to be able to read people. You remembered something a moment ago that bothered you, maybe even scared you."

He let out a chuckle but she could tell it was to hide the truth. He *had* seen something that had scared him the first time he'd laid eyes on her.

"You're going to think I'm nuts. I do."

"I might surprise you," she said. "Please. Tell me."

Marshall sighed, then met her gaze. "I saw something behind you that day. Some*one*."

"My brother?"

He shook his head. "It was a woman."

She felt the hair rise on the back of her neck. Goose bumps rippled across her flesh and it took all her willpower not to shudder. "What did this person look like?"

"This is where it gets crazy. It was a woman who looked exactly like you only…" He was the one to shudder. He laughed. "I'm sure it was probably nothing more than a shadow behind you."

"But you sensed evil."

MARSHALL OPENED HIS MOUTH to deny it. Saying it out loud would make it real. But when he looked into those amazing violet eyes of hers… "Yeah, that was the feeling I had. Something…dangerous. Or at least not of this world. Crazy, huh?"

He waited for her to tell him he'd merely been seeing things.

Instead, she chewed at her lower lip for a moment and when she lifted her glass to take a drink, he saw that her hand was shaking.

"Wait a minute. Are you telling me I really did see someone?"

She took a sip, then carefully put the glass down on the coffee table. "My mother."

He couldn't help his relief—or his embarrassment. "Your mother is here with you and your brother. I'm sorry. I can't imagine why I thought—"

"My mother's been dead for over a year."

The rest of his words froze in his throat. "Whoa. I don't know what to say."

She hesitated but only for a moment. As her gaze met his, she said, "My mother was a clairvoyant."

"A clairvoyant," he repeated.

"A fortune-teller, if you like."

"I know what a clairvoyant is."

"She specialized in reaching those who had passed over and she made a tidy sum doing it."

He heard anger in her tone. "You sound skeptical."

She shook her head. "Unfortunately, I think she might have been the real thing."

Marshall let that sink in for a moment. "That must have been interesting, growing up with a mother with that kind of…talent."

Alexa laughed. "You might say that. I was her precious daughter until I told her that I didn't have her gift. After that she centered her world around my brother."

"I'm sorry. So your brother has—"

"No." She shook her head. "He doesn't have her abilities and while I'm being honest, I didn't faint earlier today. Someone hit me."

"What?" He listened as she told him about the Crying Woman. "Why wouldn't your brother believe you?" he asked when she'd finished.

"Because he thinks I've been lying to him for years," she said and met his gaze. "My mother was convinced that I had her abilities."

"You mean that you're clairvoyant like her?"

She nodded.

"And you're not?"

She looked away and he felt his heart drop even though he'd already suspected this was what had her so terrified—not just whatever was going on over at that house.

"I'm not like her," Alexa said as she turned back to face him.

"But you're a little like her," he said carefully.

She looked as if she might try to deny it. Instead, tears filled her eyes.

He moved to sit on the couch next to her. "That's why you're so scared," he said as he reached over to take her hands in his. "The nightmares? Is that part of it?"

"I don't know. Maybe." She looked into his face. "This doesn't scare *you?*"

He laughed. "Only if you tell me that you know what I'm thinking."

She smiled through her tears. "I can't read your mind." She looked down at his large hands cradling her own. "I can't see your future either. Or my own." She sounded relieved by that and maybe a little worried.

He grinned. "That's good. Then you don't know that I've been wanting to do this since the first time I saw you." He leaned toward her and gently kissed her full mouth. Desire raced through his veins, as hot as a summer day and just as wonderful. He drew back to look into those beautiful violet eyes of hers.

She was smiling. "Maybe I *can* see the future," she said.

Marshall hoped he did too. But he felt her draw back and could see she was almost as afraid of getting involved with him as she was of that house and whatever was going on over there.

"You've been so understanding," she said. "A lot of men—"

"I'm not like a lot of men."

"No, you aren't."

"What I mean is that I don't scare off easily. Tell me about this house you're staying in."

"That's the problem. My brother doesn't just think it's haunted. He believes it is trying to kill him."

Marshall saw it then. "He thinks you can save him."

"He's wrong." She'd said it too quickly. He watched her look away, but not before he'd seen the pain in her expression and something else. Guilt.

"So they both blamed you for not having this alleged gift? Or at least not admitting that you might have it."

She smiled at his insight. "That about covers it."

He didn't think so. He had a feeling there was a lot more going on, but he was thankful she had opened up to him and didn't want to push it. She'd tell him, he hoped, when she trusted him more.

"Someone wants you to believe the house is haunted, but why?" Marshall asked.

"That's what I have to find out. I need to

know more about the Wellingtons. Can you help me?"

"I know someone you can talk to," he said. "We could go visit him tomorrow in town. Maybe have supper afterward?"

"Thank you." She touched his face, leaning in to kiss him. He kissed her again and she melted into his arms. If he had one wish, it would be that he never had to let her go.

"In the meantime," he said as the kiss ended and she rose to leave, "I don't like you staying over there."

"I can't leave. Not until I can get my brother to go as well. Maybe what we find out tomorrow will help."

He sure hoped so as he walked her to the door, because he feared what was waiting for her in that old mansion. Ghosts? Or someone who would do anything to keep the truth from coming out?

ALEXA CAREFULLY OPENED THE back door and slipped inside, glad she'd gone over to Marshall's tonight. She couldn't believe she'd confided in him. Or how relieved she was that she had.

She felt warm and happy and realized it was because he was right. He wasn't like other men. He hadn't panicked when she'd told him about her mother. Or when he'd seen what could only have been her mother standing behind her that first day.

Instead, she was the one who'd felt panic. She'd wondered how long it would be before her mother contacted her.

As if that wasn't enough to scare her off, someone wanted the people in this house, maybe especially Landon, to believe Wellington Manor was haunted. They'd been trying to run him off—and soon, she feared, herself as well.

But she was more afraid of what she'd been feeling. For Marshall Chisholm. And in this house. The sensations were growing stronger. She didn't want to admit that even to herself, though. But she knew it was part of the reason she kept fleeing to Marshall's farmhouse every night.

It wasn't just fear driving her out of Wellington Manor and sending her straight for Marshall Chisholm. She'd also needed the levelheaded cowboy more than he could know. When she'd gone up to bed tonight, she'd seen his lights on and, on impulse, had been drawn to the place, hoping that the light didn't go off before she reached it.

He and his house were a haven. She could sit in his old farmhouse with its warm essence and feel safe—and normal. She didn't feel anything in his house but peace. There hadn't been any violence inside those walls. There'd been hardship, as with any life that had lived within an old house, but there had also been an abundance of love.

While the house was definitely a draw, it was the man she'd needed to see. Desire stirred in her at the thought of him. She had always feared letting anyone get too close. But she'd never met a man quite like Marshall Chisholm. She sensed his strength, his integrity, his connection to the earth and living things.

All her senses told her this cowboy was a man she could trust—and that somehow they had become intricately linked. From the first time she'd seen him, Marshall Chisholm had gotten through the barriers she'd built around her.

With a start, Alexa realized something she hadn't first noticed when she'd stepped into Wellington Manor.

The hallway was dark.

She'd purposely left a small lamp on so she

didn't crash into anything and wake the rest of the household. Someone had turned it out.

She reached out in the pitch blackness, found the small table by the back door and cautiously felt around for the lamp. The lamp wasn't there. Why would someone—

She felt a warm hand, let out a cry and stumbled back. The lamp came on, blinding her for an instant. "Been out for another nightly run in the pasture?"

Alexa tried to still her pounding pulse as Jayden set down the lamp and turned to her. "You startled me." She pressed her hands to her heart as she realized that Jayden had seen her leave the other night as well. Still, she told herself she had nothing to fear.

But the knot on her head from earlier was a painful reminder of what she had to fear in this house. Someone knew she had found the Crying Woman device. And that someone could very easily be Jayden.

"I should warn you that I'm not the only one in this house who knows about your late-night rendezvous," Jayden said. "I get why you'd run off in the middle of the night to meet a handsome cowboy. But I don't think your brother is as understanding as I am. He seems upset that you're spending so much time away from the house."

"What does my brother think of *your* late-night rendezvous down by the pond?" she asked before she could bite her tongue.

Jayden's eyes narrowed. "Touché. Apparently I'm not the only one who has been keeping an eye on what goes on around here. Is that why your brother invited you to come stay with us? To spy on us?"

"I'm not here to spy on anyone," she snapped. "I just don't want to see my brother hurt."

There was almost a sadness to his smile. "I'm afraid it's too late for that."

Before she could ask what he meant, Jayden turned and strode down the dark hallway.

Alexa stared after him, more convinced than ever that she needed to get her brother out of this house—and herself as well. The longer she stayed here, the harder it would be to keep lying to herself—let alone Landon—about what she was sensing among them.

She was relieved when she reached her room and quickly locked the door behind her. She desperately wanted to talk to her brother away from this house—and his wife. But that wasn't going to happen if Sierra had anything to do with it.

As she stepped toward her bed, she saw the tray with milk and cookies—and the note. She felt her heart soften when she recognized Landon's neat script.

Alexa,
I'm sorry. Tomorrow let's get away from here and talk.
Love,
Landon

Relief and love for her brother made tears well in her eyes. If they could get away from Sierra and this house, maybe she could talk some sense into him. He was right about one thing. There was something in this house controlling him. But Alexa knew it was flesh and blood—not some avenging spirit.

She smiled as she sat down on the edge of the bed and picked up one of the cookies. Chocolate chip, her favorite. Landon remembered.

She took a bite. The cookie was delicious. When she was little, her father would have the housekeeper bake cookies for her in secret. Tallulah didn't like her eating sugar, especially right before she went to bed. She swore it was the cause of Alexa's nightmares. But her father called that poppycock and snuck cookies and milk in to her. They would share them and talk about their day. It was the best of her childhood memories.

Alexa wished she and Landon had shared the same father, since his had been little more than a sperm donor. She'd tried to make up for what he'd missed, not having a father, by baking chocolate chip cookies and sneaking them and milk in to her brother at night after their mother had gone to bed.

Touched by her brother's thoughtfulness, she finished the cookies and milk. But as she started to get ready for bed, she suddenly felt lightheaded. A terrible thought wove itself through her muddled conscious. *No.* She lunged for the phone on the nightstand. It was the last thing she remembered.

Chapter Eight

The next morning Marshall drove to the Chisholm Cattle Company main ranch house. He was worried about his folks since hearing the news. He still couldn't believe that Aggie Wells had escaped. He was also feeling a little guilty about the amount of time he'd been taking off to work on his house—and most recently, to spend with Alexa.

Last night after Alexa had left, he'd gotten back on the computer and called up a list of psychics. It hadn't taken long to find Tallulah Cross. Alexa had played down just how famous her mother had been and how often her predictions had been right.

What had really bowled him over though was the photograph he'd found of Alexa's mother. The two could have been twins. He'd felt a chill in the warm room. The woman was the same one he swore he'd seen standing behind Alexa the first time he'd seen her.

Scrolling down, he'd found Tallulah Cross's obituary and seen that Alexa and Landon were mentioned. What would it have been like to have a clairvoyant for a mother? He and his brothers wouldn't have been able to get away with anything.

Instead, Marshall had spent his life without a mother. Emma was as close to a real mother as he'd had. He'd either been too young or his father's other wives had lasted such a short time, he couldn't remember them.

Hoyt had been both mother and father though, doing the best he could, which was damned good. When the boys had gotten older, he'd always seemed to be one step ahead of them. It wasn't until Marshall was grown that he realized the reason his father always had known what mischief he and his brothers had gotten into. His father had gotten into the same mischief when he was young.

"Hey, stranger," his brother Logan said as he came into the kitchen. He could smell blueberry muffins and made a beeline for them and a mug of coffee. Everyone was seated about the big kitchen table. His brothers were elbowing each other, snickering. "How're the new neighbors?"

He shot Tanner a look, wishing he hadn't

confided in him. His brother held up his hands and looked confused as if he didn't have any idea what Marshall was upset about.

"How's the house coming along?" his father asked.

"Slowly," he said, feeling guilty that he hadn't worked on it much since meeting Alexa Cross. "I could use a few more days, if that won't put too much pressure on the rest of you."

There were moans and groans but his father said not to worry, take what time he needed.

"With his mind on *other* things, he's pretty worthless anyway," Tanner joked.

Marshall felt Emma's gaze on him. If anyone was clairvoyant, it was Emma McDougal Chisholm. Earlier, she'd seemed distracted with her own problems—Aggie Wells being on the loose again. He could tell that his father was anxious as well about Emma's safety.

As the rest of the family cleared out, Hoyt saying he would be in the barn but not to leave without saying goodbye, Emma said, "So who is she?"

Marshall started to play dumb, but knew he'd be wasting his time. "Her name's Alexa Cross. She's staying over at Wellington Manor."

Emma lifted a brow.

"Sierra Wellington married her brother, Landon. They're remodeling the old place, thinking of making it in to a bed-and-breakfast."

"Tell me about this Alexa."

He smiled, unable not to. "She's amazing. She's gorgeous, smart…" He shook his head, realizing he could go on forever about her.

"So what's the problem?" Emma asked.

"There isn't—"

"Something's wrong. Tell me. That is why you're here this morning, isn't it?"

It amazed him how she could see through all of them, maybe especially Hoyt. "I was also worried about you."

"Thank you, I appreciate that," Emma said. "Now pour us another cup of coffee and tell me what's wrong."

"It's kind of complicated. Alexa's brother thinks the house is haunted. I'm not one to hold much stock in all that, but…"

"You've *seen* something?"

He nodded. "The first time I saw Alexa there was a woman standing behind her. Turns out it was her mother—who's been dead for a year."

Emma shivered in spite of her next words. "It must have been a trick of the light."

"Yeah, that's what I said, but it turns out her mother was a clairvoyant. I looked her up on the internet. She was a famous psychic."

"And her daughter?" Emma asked.

Yes, that was the question, wasn't it? "I can't be sure but I think she might be as well, though she doesn't like the idea and doesn't want to be clairvoyant. Something is going on with her and that house and her brother and maybe even her mother. I know that sounds crazy."

Emma shook her head.

"What?" he asked.

"It's you Chisholms. You all prefer women in trouble."

ALEXA WOKE TO DAYLIGHT, a horrible nightmare following her up from the darkness. She sat up, shocked to find herself still fully dressed and on the floor. Next to her was the broken plate and glass that had held the cookies and milk. She must have knocked them off the tray as she fell.

She leaned against the bed, her head swimming, as she tried to remember what had happened. Had someone hit her again? The last thing she remembered was eating the cookies and milk that Landon had left her.

The thought froze in her mind. Landon's note. He hadn't mentioned the cookies and milk. Or had he?

Alexa got to her feet, found the note on the tray and reread it. Her head ached and she felt sick to her stomach. Landon *hadn't* mentioned the cookies and milk. He would have—had he been the one to leave them. But who else could have known about the ritual?

Sierra. Of course Landon would have told her.

Alexa had to sit down on the edge of the bed for a moment, her head spinning. *Her brother's wife had drugged her?* She was going to be sick! She made a mad dash for the bathroom, barely making it before she threw up.

Feeling a little better, she turned on the shower, stripped off her clothes and stepped under the hot spray. She still felt awful, but this was more heartsick. Her brother had no idea whom he'd married, *what* he'd married.

Why would Sierra drug her?

Had her intention been to scare Alexa off? Or had she hoped for a drug overdose that killed her?

She had just come out of the shower when she heard the tap on her door. Last night she'd had the good sense to lock the door but anyone with a skeleton key could open any room in this house.

"Alexa?" Gigi called. "I just wanted to come up and check on you. Landon was worried, but Sierra said to let you sleep."

Oh, she did, did she?

Alexa glanced at the clock. It was almost two in the afternoon! She'd slept all night and most of the day?

"I'm fine. I was just being lazy and I had a book I wanted to finish," she improvised. "I'm getting ready to take a shower."

Gigi sounded relieved. "No problem. I'll let your brother know. When he called and I told him we hadn't seen you, he asked me to come check. He and Sierra are on their way back from town, but he'll be glad that you're relaxing. We were just about to eat a late lunch."

"Tell everyone to go ahead and eat without me. I'm not really hungry. I'll come down later and get something."

"All right."

Alexa waited until she heard Gigi's footfalls recede down the hall before she checked to make sure the hallway was empty. It was. She closed the door and locked it again.

The last thing she wanted was food. Her stomach was still roiling, especially after hearing that Sierra hadn't wanted Gigi to wake her. At least Landon had been concerned enough to send someone up, she thought, as she looked at the clock and realized Marshall would be picking her up soon.

She had felt guilty last night about researching Sierra's family. Now she was more determined than ever to find out everything she could about the Wellingtons.

As she started to get dressed, she noticed the book beside her bed had been moved. She quickly picked it up as she remembered the partially burned papers she'd put under it. They were gone.

EMMA HAD BEEN WALKING around on eggshells since almost getting caught yesterday on the phone with Aggie.

"I wondered where you'd gone," Hoyt had said when she'd opened the bathroom door and found him standing there. "The boys are leaving. I knew you'd want to say goodbye. Do you feel all right?"

She'd known she'd looked suspicious. "My stomach is a little upset."

He'd pulled her into his arms, making her feel guilty again. But her stomach had been upset, so she hadn't really lied.

She'd almost confessed everything, but she knew her husband. He would never let her meet Aggie, especially alone, if he knew what she was up to.

Now with her stepsons gone, she could sense Hoyt's impatience to get back to ranch work and his real life. She felt the same way.

"I think I'll make some cookies," she said. Baking was the only thing keeping her sane.

"What kind of cookies?" Hoyt asked, coming up behind her as she creamed the butter and sugar for the cookies in her large mixer.

"Your favorite, snickerdoodles."

He planted a kiss on her neck. She was grateful for the amazing intimacy they shared. But as she glanced at the clock, she knew she couldn't let him talk her into going upstairs for even a quickie. She needed to meet Aggie and the sooner the better.

"Any chance of leaving that for a little while?" he asked as he put his arms around her and snuggled closer.

Oh, she was tempted. But feared she might not be able to get away later. "I can't really leave these ingredients right now. Don't you need to check on that mare of yours again? I should have the first batch done by the time you get back."

She could tell he had other things on his mind than his horses and he didn't want to leave her alone, even though he'd only be out in the barn nearby. "What did the vet say when he came out and had a look at her?" she asked.

"He thought she had an infection in that one leg. He gave her something for it. Maybe I'd better go see how she's doing. I won't be long."

"Take your time. I'll yell if I need you."

He studied her for a long moment. "Maybe when I get back…"

She smiled as she leaned in to kiss him, then quickly turned around. "Let me finish my cookies."

"I don't know what I would do without you, Emma. It would kill me," he said behind her.

Guilt gnawed at her. She didn't dare turn around. "You won't ever have to find out."

"I hope not," he said.

Out of the corner of her eye, she saw him

take his Stetson off the peg on the wall where he'd tossed it earlier. As he set it on his thick, graying blond hair, he said, "See you shortly."

The moment she heard the front door close behind him, Emma ripped off her apron and stepped to the doorway to make sure he hadn't forgotten something and was headed back.

Emma watched him striding toward the barn, thinking how blessed she was to have such a wonderful man. Guilt ate her up as she left the cookie dough and hurried out the back door, running down the trail to disappear into the woods.

ALEXA HAD JUST FINISHED getting dressed when she heard footfalls. At first she thought it was someone coming down the hall.

Then she realized they were coming from overhead. Someone was on the third floor. The footsteps had stopped. Now whoever it was seemed to be moving things around as if searching for something.

If everyone was down having breakfast, then who was upstairs?

Grabbing her room key, she decided to find out.

The broom closet was locked—just as it

had been the other time. Alexa used her skeleton key from her room to open it and quickly stepped inside, closing and locking the door behind her.

She stood for a moment, listening. Hearing nothing beyond the panel door, she carefully slid it open, stepped through and closed it behind her. She had to feel her way to the stairs since she had no flashlight. Once she started up them, though, she could see faint light bleeding in through a space under the door at the top of the stairs. She had her key ready, but found the door to be unlocked.

Cautiously, she opened it. As the door swung open, she saw that at least this part of the third floor was as Sierra had described it.

The floor seemed full of old furniture and boxes. She could hear someone moving around at the other end of the room—directly over Alexa's room. The person appeared to still be looking for something.

Stepping behind one of the larger boxes, she eased herself through the furniture, boxes and old trunks until she was so close that she could hear the person breathing hard on the other side of a line of tall bureaus.

She tried to move one of the tallboys to peek through to see who it was. The leg of the bureau scraped on the hardwood floor, making a squeaking sound.

The person on the other side froze. Alexa did the same for a moment, then realizing she'd been caught, stood and tried to push her way through.

But by the time she slipped between the tallboy and an old buffet, whoever had been rummaging around was gone, his or her footfalls quickly receding.

Alexa glanced around, curious what the person had been looking for. With a start, she saw two dark eyes staring at her from one of the boxes. As she stepped closer, she saw with a chill that someone had poked the eyes out of a doll with a sharp object that had left cut marks around the eye holes.

Unable to look away, as if at a car wreck, she reached for the doll. The moment her fingers touched it, she felt a tingle run up her arm and quickly jerked back from what flashed in her mind.

She'd seen a little girl in a pretty pink-and-white dress, a matching bow in her hair. There was blood on the girl's dress....

As she felt a small tug on the hem of her skirt, Alexa had to cover her mouth with her hand to keep from screaming. She jerked away, the fabric pulling tightly before swinging back against her legs.

She stood staring in the dim light at the empty space next to her. There was no little girl. It was all just— A ball rolled across the floor.

Alexa stumbled back against an old bureau. She had to grip the edge to keep from falling as the ball rolled past her. Her elbow caught on one of the boxes. It tumbled to the floor with a crash.

Old black-and-white photographs spilled out of it and across the floor.

Trying to get a grip on her panic, Alexa reached down to pick up the spilled photographs. One caught her eye. She lifted it from the floor and felt her heart stop.

The photo was an old one, the paper cracked and faded, but the image was a young woman, the resemblance to Sierra more than startling.

The woman was dressed in an old-fashioned dress, high-button boots, a fur stole around her slim shoulders. Her blond hair was piled high on her head, exposing a long, graceful neck and accenting her high cheekbones and stunning beauty. Around the woman's neck was an unusual necklace, the pendant hanging from a thick chain appearing to have something written on it.

Alexa squinted at the photo, trying to read the words.

"My great-great-grandmother," Sierra said, appearing out of nowhere.

Startled, Alexa dropped the photograph. It fell to the floor with a whisper of sound. "I'm sorry. I was—"

"I know what you were doing," Sierra said as she moved to pick up the spilled box of photos from the floor. There was coldness in her voice, anger. She glanced at the scrape in the floor where Alexa had moved the bureau aside, then at her sister-in-law. Her blue eyes could have been chipped from ice for all the warmth in them.

"You're digging into my family's history, trying to frighten my husband," she said, a warning in her tone.

"He was frightened before I got here."

Sierra cocked her head, as if listening to a voice Alexa couldn't hear. "You don't like me, do you?"

Alexa was taken aback by the bluntness of her question. "I'm concerned about your relationship with my brother."

"That doesn't answer my question."

"I want him to be happy."

"What makes you think he isn't happy?" Sierra idly picked up the photo of her great-great-grandmother and studied it as if looking at her own photo, searching it for a flaw in her beauty and finding none. "I'm his wife. He loves me."

Sierra placed the photograph carefully in the box on top of the others, then looked at Alexa almost as if she'd forgotten she was still in the room. "I think it might be time for you to leave. You really shouldn't be gone too long from your job. I'm sure if you tell Landon—"

"I'm not leaving until I find out what is going on in this house," Alexa said with surprising firmness.

It seemed to surprise Sierra as well. She let out a laugh. "So you aren't as meek as you pretend."

"When it comes to my brother—"

"Yes. Well, for his sake, I want you to leave. You don't want anything to happen to him, do you?"

Alexa was suddenly shaking inside. "That sounds like a threat."

Sierra laughed. "Why would I threaten Landon? I love him."

"Do you?"

Her sister-in-law's gaze narrowed. "I won't have you coming between me and my husband, that's all I'm saying. Don't make him choose between his love for you and his love for me, because you will lose."

With that, she turned and left.

Alexa stood, trembling with rage and fear, as she watched the young woman go.

Chapter Nine

Everyone was gathered around the kitchen table when Alexa came downstairs. She saw that Landon had his arm around his wife. Sierra looked upset and Alexa guessed that she'd tattled on her to Landon.

"What's going on?" Alexa asked in the heavy silence she'd walked into.

"It's Carolina," Devlin said from the end of the table. "She's going back to California."

Alexa felt her heart drop. Was this because of that stupid palm reading last night?

"Look, it's all my fault," Jayden said. "I shouldn't have said anything about babies. I had no idea—"

"No, if anyone is to blame, it's me," Archer said, getting to his feet. "I knew how badly she wanted a baby and she knew I didn't want kids. We were bound to get to this point. It's been coming for a long time."

"You aren't going too, are you?" Sierra asked.

Archer nodded his head. "She's making arrangements, but the earliest flight she can get is the day after tomorrow."

Alexa was glad he wasn't going to leave Carolina alone, given what she'd seen when she'd taken the young woman's hand last night.

"I saved you some lunch," Landon said to his sister, letting go of Sierra to head to the stove.

She couldn't miss the way Sierra looked at her. A mixture of anger and jealousy. She wanted Landon all to herself. But how far did that need of hers go? All the way to murder?

"Thank you, but I have a date for supper later," Alexa said as she joined her brother at the stove.

Landon raised a brow. "With that *cowboy* again?"

She bristled at the way he said "cowboy." It sounded like something Sierra would say.

"At least taste this," her brother said shoving a spoonful of meatloaf toward her. "It tastes just like Mother used to make."

Meatloaf was one of the few things their mother did cook. "Yes, it does taste like hers."

Her stomach roiled. She didn't need the meat-loaf—or the reminder.

"He doesn't wait on me like that," Sierra said as she started to clean off the table.

"Sierra," Alexa said, loud enough for everyone to hear. "I wanted to thank you for the cookies and milk you left beside my bed last night."

"You left her cookies and milk?" Landon asked, surprise and pleasure in his tone as he stepped back over to the table.

"No," Sierra said and blinked her big baby blues. "It wasn't me."

"Oh?" Alexa said. "They were chocolate chip cookies. I thought Landon must have told you about a tradition we had as children."

Her brother was studying his wife, not quite as sure now. "You remember me telling you how Alexa would sneak me cookies? Mother hated us eating any sugar. Chocolate chip cookies were my favorite and Alexa's."

"You might have mentioned it," Sierra conceded, clearly flustered. "But I didn't leave her cookies and milk. I'm sorry I didn't think of it."

"Strange. I wonder who did?" Alexa said and glanced around the table at Archer, Gigi and Jayden. They all shook their heads.

"I have no idea who left them," Sierra snapped.

"Landon, did you mention our tradition to anyone else?" Alexa asked and saw him start to shake his head.

"*I* probably did," Sierra said quickly. "It was so sweet, I'm sure I shared it with someone, maybe Carolina." She turned to her husband. "It's my day to clean up the dishes. You should see if you can help Devlin."

"Actually," Alexa said. "Why don't you go see if Carolina's all right? Landon and I will do the dishes."

Sierra started to object, but Landon cut her off.

"It will give Alexa and me a chance to talk."

Sierra's face was a mask of fury, but she worked up a smile for Landon, gave him a quick kiss on the cheek and shot Alexa a hateful look before she flounced out, Archer, Gigi and Jayden leaving as well.

"You HAVE A DATE AND ARE definitely not doing dishes," Landon said after they were alone in the kitchen. "But I'd love it if you kept me company while I did them. I was worried about you when Gigi said you hadn't been downstairs all day. Are you all right?"

She was touched by his concern.

He turned to face her. "I think I know what this is about. Listen, I'm sorry, sis. I love you. It wasn't fair what I did to you, getting you here and then expecting you to—"

"It's all right," Alexa said, feeling awful. "I do want to help you, Landon, any way I can."

"I know." He gave her a hug and the two of them began to clear the table. It felt again like the way it had when they were kids. They'd been inseparable. Was that her problem with Sierra? Was she just jealous that she was no longer the most important person in Landon's life anymore?

"I'm concerned about what is going on in this house," Alexa said as they dumped the dishes in a tub of hot, soapy water.

She wasn't sure how to broach the subject with him, but he had to know. "Sierra probably mentioned that I was up on the third floor earlier."

"Sis, we told you how dangerous—"

"There was someone else up there going through boxes. I didn't get a look at the person, but whoever it was heard a noise and quickly left. Was everyone downstairs when you and Sierra returned?"

He frowned. "Everyone but Carolina. Archer told us that they'd had an argument and she was leaving."

Why, if that were true, would she have been going through boxes up on the third floor? Was it possible the argument had been a ruse?

"What difference does it make who was up there going through boxes? Maybe they were just curious. Or maybe what you heard wasn't even a person."

"Landon, there is something going on that has nothing to do with ghosts. You and the others haven't heard the Crying Woman again, have you? Someone wants you all to *believe* there are ghosts in this house. If we knew why, then maybe we would know why you keep having these *accidents*."

"I've been thinking about that," he said quietly, checking over his shoulder to make sure they were still alone. "A haunted bed-and-breakfast might bring in more people than one that isn't."

Relief swept over her. He *had* believed her and given it some thought. "You think Sierra might have been behind the Crying Woman."

"Or one of her friends. It isn't like any harm was done," he added quickly.

"When I found the device, someone hit me and left me lying out in the hallway, Landon," she said.

"They obviously panicked."

She wanted to shake him. "You suspected something or someone was responsible for your accidents when you called me to come out here. You wouldn't have done that if you hadn't been suspicious."

Before he could argue the point, she said, "My getting hit wasn't the only incident. Whoever left me the milk and cookies…they drugged them. I woke up on the floor."

He shook his head. "No. I can't imagine who would do something like that. It wasn't Sierra. You heard her—she swore it wasn't her."

Alexa said nothing as he laid the dish towel on the counter and sat down at the closest chair. Resting his elbows on the table, he put his head in his hands.

She took a chair next to him and put her hand on his shoulder. "It's not just you someone is trying to get rid of now. We have to find out why."

Alexa heard the doorbell and glanced at

her watch. Her date. "I have to go," she said to her brother, squeezing his shoulder. "Just think about what I've said."

Landon nodded solemnly as the doorbell rang again. "I want to meet your date."

"Yes," Sierra said from the kitchen doorway. "We all do."

IT WAS SHADY AND COOL in the cottonwoods along the Milk River. The river was narrow and deep where it cut through the Chisholm ranch, the water dark and surprisingly fast-moving along this section of the river.

Emma hadn't gone far when she saw Aggie step out of the trees and onto the path.

She felt her heart leap in her chest and, as she watched Aggie reach into the shoulder bag she carried, she feared she'd made a fatal mistake agreeing to this.

For one heart-stopping moment, Emma thought Aggie was about to pull a gun from her purse and slowed to a stop a few yards away, moving only when she realized how foolish she'd been as Aggie pulled out a large manila envelope.

"Are you all right?" Aggie asked, no doubt seeing her initial panic.

Emma nodded and joined the woman. "A little spooked."

Aggie laughed. "You have to trust me."

"I'm trying," she said as the woman laid the large envelope in her hands.

She opened the envelope and took out one of the surveillance photos. It had been shot from a distance with a telephoto lens, from the look of it.

The woman in the photo was in her early fifties, lean and pretty, with medium-length dark hair that accented her dark eyes.

"Well?" Aggie asked.

Emma had seen a photograph of Laura after she'd insisted that Hoyt must have one. He'd dug out a box of old photographs from the basement.

It took him a while, but he'd finally produced one of Laura. She'd been a beautiful redhead with long, luxurious hair and big, blue eyes.

"The hair and eye color is wrong," Emma said.

Aggie gave her an impatient look. "Hair dye and contacts. Do you really think she could have stayed hidden all these years if she had stayed a blue-eyed redhead? She would have stuck out like a sore thumb. But the way she looks now, I really doubt anyone in Whitehorse would recognize her. She wasn't from here and few would remember her, since she and Hoyt weren't married that long."

Laura Chisholm had been beautiful. No wonder Hoyt had fallen for her. Emma felt a hard jab of jealousy. And she had been a redhead too.

"Look at her face," Aggie ordered. "The cheekbones, the shape of the eyes. Here." She reached into the envelope and brought out another photo. "It's a computerized age-progression photo of what Laura Chisholm would look like if she were still alive. I had a friend in law enforcement make it for me."

Emma was reminded that Aggie had a lot of friends. That was how she'd been able to avoid the mental hospital. She stared at the surveillance photo, then the computerized photo. The women could have been twins. "What is this woman's name?"

"She goes by Sharon Jones. Her address is in the envelope. She lives in Billings—just three hours away—and guess what? Sharon Jones didn't exist until four months ago—just about the time you married Hoyt."

Emma felt a chill at the thought that the person who might want her dead could be just three hours away. Or, just inches away, if she was wrong about Aggie, she reminded herself.

"Do you believe me now?" Aggie demanded.

"I have to admit, there is a remarkable resemblance," Emma said. "Aggie, you need to take this to the police in Billings," she continued, trying to hand the photos and envelopes back to her.

"I told you, no police. We're doing this together. It's your life that's at stake as well as mine. I don't trust the police not to blow this. If Laura disappears again, the next time you see her will be the day she kills you. Me, I'll be in the loony bin if the police don't get a confession out of her. But you and I—" Aggie suddenly broke off midsentence.

"You didn't tell anyone you were meeting me back here, did you?" Aggie demanded.

"No, I snuck out."

Aggie swore. "You called the sheriff."

"No." Emma turned and saw several deputies moving through the trees.

"You're going to get yourself killed!" Aggie cried, shoving the manila envelope with the photographs at her before turning to run.

"Stop!" A gunshot boomed.

Emma heard Aggie cry out as she stumbled and fell into the river. As she stared in shock, the deputies and sheriff came running up, followed moments later by Hoyt.

Emma could only stare at the spot where Aggie had gone under and hadn't come up again.

MARSHALL KNEW SOMETHING was wrong the moment Alexa answered the door. He'd been smiling before that, but now whispered, "Are you okay?" She looked pale and her eyes weren't their usual brilliant violet.

"Why don't you come in," she said tightly. "Everyone wants to meet you."

Everyone? "Great," he said, tugging off his Stetson, then he wiped his feet and stepped into the mansion.

He'd known it would be impressive inside but still he was taken aback by how grandiose the interior had once been. Its looks had faded, but it was still beautiful. He took the opulence all in and let out a low whistle.

"High praise," Sierra said and stepped forward. "I'm Sierra Wellington. I'm glad you like my house."

"Wellington Cross," a man behind her corrected. He looked enough like Alexa that

Marshall figured he was Landon even before he introduced himself.

The others were quickly introduced. Gigi, the former cheerleader, and no doubt, the most popular girl at school. Archer, the former jock. Devlin, the smug rich kid. Jayden, the odd man out. Only Carolina was missing.

He noticed that Alexa's brother looked uncomfortable and could understand now why Alexa felt the need to protect Landon. Marshall understood it even more after meeting Landon's wife. Under all that blond, blue-eyed, innocent exterior, Sierra was as cold as this house.

"So how many cattle do you have on your ranch?" Devlin asked.

"I couldn't say offhand," Marshall answered. It was impolite to ask a rancher how many cattle he ran. It was like asking someone how much he was worth.

"You probably have hired hands to do all the real work, right?" Archer asked.

"No, my brothers and I and our father work the ranch. We actually like getting our hands dirty," Marshall said.

"I apologize for them," Alexa said after they were seated in his pickup.

"You don't need to apologize for them," he said. "They aren't *your* friends."

"No," she agreed quickly.

"They're not your brother's either."

She glanced over at him. "You felt that as well?"

He nodded as he started the pickup and drove toward town.

"I keep telling myself they're young."

"Not that much younger than us. They're spoiled rich kids. I got the feeling your brother doesn't like them any more than you do."

"Does it show?"

He laughed. "No, you both hide it well. So that bunch is remodeling the mansion?" He couldn't help sounding skeptical.

"Apparently, though they work odd hours. They must work late at night since no one gets up early. I really don't know what they're doing."

He saw her frown. "Something else happen?"

She turned toward him, her expression softening. "Last night someone left me milk and cookies. I thought it was my brother because there was a note there from him and chocolate chip cookies and milk were a tradition when we were kids. They were drugged. I woke up on the floor—a couple of hours ago."

"Alexa," he said, unconsciously hitting the brakes as he reached over for her.

"I'm all right. They didn't give me enough drugs to kill me so I'm pretty sure they are just trying to scare me off."

He swore, terrified of what they might try next. He said as much to her as he saw White-horse in the distance, the tall cottonwoods marking the Milk River's trail past the small Montana town.

"That's why I have to know as much as possible about the Wellington family history. It doesn't make any sense why anyone would want me out of that house unless…"

"Unless?" he asked.

"My sister-in-law seems to be rather jealous of my relationship with my brother."

"So much so that she drugged you?"

"Possibly. I saw Jayden, the single man at the house, with one of the wives. It could have been Sierra, which would explain why she might want to get rid of my brother. That and his inheritance. And I have a feeling Sierra hasn't been honest about her past."

Yep, a viper's nest, Marshall thought as he pulled into the yard of an old house on the river on what locals called Millionaire Row. The houses were modest by most standards, two to three stories and wood framed. This one had a large shop next to it, where he figured they would find the owner.

"You sure you're up for this?" he asked as Alexa rubbed her temples.

She nodded, although he could see it hurt her head to do so.

Marshall led her toward the large metal shop building to meet a friend of his father's who had roots that ran back to before the railroad cut across this part of Montana.

"Hey, Little Chisholm," Dave called as they stepped into the cavernous building. He'd been calling all six of the brothers that since they were kids and his father used to bring them here on visits. He wiped his hands on a rag and stood from where he'd been working on a large lawn mower.

Marshall used to love to come over to Dave's shop in the winter to sit by the woodstove and listen to his father and Dave talk hunting and fishing, the weather and what was going on locally. Dave usually knew everything going on. Marshall recalled many tall tales that got kicked around this building over the years.

"Dave, this is my friend Alexa Cross," he said by way of introduction. "She is interested in the Wellington family."

DAVE, A WIRY OLD MAN WITH a shock of white hair and intense blue eyes, smiled. "You one of them staying out there at the mansion?"

Alexa nodded, even though it hurt to do so. "Anything you can tell me would be greatly appreciated."

He studied her for a moment as if sizing her up, then invited them to sit in one of the mismatched chairs around a desk at the back. "You're not a relation, are you?" he asked as he walked over to an antique soda pop machine. "Coke or Dr. Pepper, those are your choices."

"No, I'm not a relative," Alexa said.

"I'll take a Coke," Marshall said and looked over at Alexa. She nodded. "Alexa will too."

"Wouldn't want to tell you anything if you were," Dave said with a shake of his head as he brought them each a Coke and a Dr. Pepper for himself. "Nasty business, those Wellingtons."

"So you knew the family?" Marshall asked.

Dave let out a chortle as he sat down behind his desk and leaned back in the chair. The desk was covered with papers, just as the shed was full of anything and everything a person could imagine. The heads of antelope, elk and deer lined the walls, along with old calendars and other memorabilia, including probably every metal license plate Dave and his family had ever owned.

"Now that was one scary family," Dave was saying. "I heard one of them had inherited the house. What's this one like?"

Marshall looked to Alexa. "How would you describe her?"

"Her?" Dave raised a brow.

"She is the great-great-granddaughter of the original builder," Alexa said.

"That would be Jedidiah Wellington. Growing up, I heard all kinds of stories about that old man. You've seen the house. He brought in German craftsmen to build it. Spent a small fortune. Craziest thing anyone had ever seen the way he designed it."

"Was it originally planned as a hotel?" Alexa asked.

Dave shook his head. "More like a lodge. He was going to bring in Europeans to hunt down in the Missouri Breaks and up into that wild country to the north of the Chisholm place."

"What happened to change his mind?" Marshall asked.

"His daughter hung herself in one of the rooms upstairs. She'd gotten pregnant by a local cowboy, had the baby and supposedly, because the man wouldn't marry her, killed herself."

"There were rumors that Jedidiah killed her in a rage for having a bastard child."

"What happened to the baby?" she asked with a shudder.

"The wife was raising it. Then one night she came into town, hysterical, said the baby had been kidnapped. The infant was later found smothered to death in the basement. No one ever believed the baby had been taken, but they had no proof that someone in the house had done it. No kidnapper was ever caught. Figure the wife or Jedidiah killed it. The wife went mad after that, had to be locked up in one of the rooms. My grandfather said the wailing was unbearable. There'd been a small town there. But the railroad was coming through about then. They all moved away, wanting to get as far away from that kind of trouble as they could."

"That's horrible," Alexa said, thinking that it explained the Crying Woman device she'd found behind the wall. Someone at that house knew the Wellington's history, just as she had suspected. "She died in the house?"

"Yep. Sierra and Jedidiah had a son too," Dave said and stopped talking abruptly at the sound of Alexa's sudden intake of breath. "Something wrong?"

"No, I'm sorry. It's just that the woman who inherited the house, her name is Sierra," Alexa said, thinking of the old photograph and the resemblance to the current Sierra.

"Probably named after her great-great-grandmother," Dave said, as if he didn't see anything strange about that.

Named after a woman who went crazy in the house that Sierra Wellington Cross now wanted to live? Alexa took a drink of the icy cold soda pop in her hand, her hand shaking.

Dave got back into his rhythm again. "Jedidiah gave up on his plan to make it a hunting lodge, closed off a lot of the rooms, lived there with his son. Some family and servants came and went over that time. Rumors circulated about the horrible things that went on in that house. The son, I think his name was John, married. His young wife died during a hard winter. Froze to death just yards from the house. John said she'd gone out to check the chickens, but everyone believed she was trying to flee that house, fell and died in a snowdrift."

Dave took a sip of his soda pop. "She left behind a son who grew up and lived in the old place for a while. He was named after his grandfather, Jedidiah. Jed left, and no one saw him for years. By the time he came back, the rest of them were dead and buried."

Jed Wellington, Alexa realized, would have been Sierra's grandfather.

"Brought his wife and kids, a son and daughter. Daughter fell down an old well and died. Son left when he was old enough. He only came back a couple of times. I suspect the only reason was because of the scandal hanging over his head. Came back here to hide out."

"What scandal was that?" Marshall asked.

Dave took another drink, clearly relishing the story of the Wellingtons. "Money. Not sure of the specifics. I just know he stole a bunch of it from someone. Heard later that he killed himself."

Alexa stared at the old man as she realized he must be talking about Sierra's father. "What was this Wellington's name?"

"Went by J. A.Wellington. I had the newspaper clipping. Not sure what happened to it."

"What happened to the house?" Marshall asked.

"Some old-maid niece moved in with what family was left. She was the last to die there. Hardly anyone had seen her for years."

Dave chuckled. "Did hear one great story about old Jed. Wrecked his car one night on the road out to his place. Swore to the sheriff and old doc that he was being chased by a phantom pickup—and it wasn't the first time either."

"A phantom pickup?" Marshall asked and chuckled. "Sounds to me like old Jed got into the sauce."

"Swore he hadn't had a thing to drink," Dave said. "After that there were occasionally stories about a pickup chasing teenagers out on that road late at night. Said the truck would almost run them off the road and then just up and disappear."

Alexa was still thinking about Sierra's father killing himself after some sort of scandal. She couldn't help but feel sympathy for her sister-in-law. She knew what it was like to grow up without a father.

"That family certainly met with a lot of

tragedy," Marshall said, glancing over at her. She saw concern in his gaze and felt another heartstring sing. "Thanks for telling us everything, Dave."

"Yes. Thank you for the information," Alexa said as she got to her feet.

"A lot of hair-raising stories have come out of *that* house and the people who have lived there," Dave said. "Kids still tell tales about seeing things out there at night, including that old pickup trying to run them off the road. In their cases, though I'm sure alcohol was involved. Still, you couldn't get me to stay in that house for any amount of money."

"You believe in ghosts?" Alexa asked, surprised that he would.

"I believe in evil," Dave said as he chucked his empty soda can into a large trash container by the back door. "They say that when there is a violent death, the soul lingers. That's unholy ground out there. Someone should have burned that place down years ago. Take some dynamite to it."

"You all right?" Marshall asked as they left.

"I guess I'm not surprised." She'd sensed a dark past in the house, though she was shaken by what she'd learned. "Someone else in that house knows the history."

"The Crying Woman," he said. "You think it was meant to be the original Sierra Wellington."

She shivered at the thought that the *latest* Sierra might be behind all of this, since she would be the most likely to know the Wellington history.

But how could she use her family's tragedies? Why would she?

Chapter Ten

Marshall had been wonderful at supper, but after everything she'd learned about her sister-in-law's family, Alexa hadn't been a very good date.

"I'm sorry I wasn't much fun tonight," she said as they left the restaurant.

"Hey, I just enjoy being with you," he said, smiling at her as he led her to his pickup. "I know you have a lot on your mind."

"I can't get my mind off the Wellington family's tragic history."

"Will you tell your brother about his wife's family?" Marshall asked as they left Whitehorse and headed north along the Milk River. It had gotten dark. The headlights of the pickup cut a swath of light through the blackness.

"I don't know. I doubt he'll see anything pertinent about the information. He's blind when it comes to Sierra. He won't want to admit that she might be anything like her family. According to Sierra, she was raised by her single mother. Depending on when her father killed himself, she might not even be able to remember him."

"Your brother could have a point. How much of who we are can we blame on our genes? I never knew my biological father, barely remember my mother. I consider Hoyt Chisholm my father. He raised me with his values. I believe I'm the man I am because of him."

Alexa smiled over at him. She liked the man he was. But she could argue the part genetics played since she didn't just look like her mother. She had fought everything about her mother's life and yet here she was, her mother's daughter, cursed with at least some of her mother's gift. Wasn't it just as possible that a bad gene could be handed down? A criminal gene?

"Sierra certainly comes from an interesting gene pool," Alexa said. "I'd like to know more about her mother. Actually more about Sierra and her father."

"It probably wouldn't hurt to learn more about *everyone* living there right now, given what's happened to you," Marshall said.

He had a point. She wouldn't mind knowing more about all of the people in that house.

"What are you going to do if you can't talk your brother into leaving?"

"I don't know. Eventually I have to get back to work." Alexa looked out her side window. She had a job, an apartment, and she supposed that would be considered a life. But it had always felt temporary. Journalists moved around a lot, from paper to paper. She'd just assumed she would too until she could quit and write children's books. That was her dream.

"I'm sure you're anxious to get back," Marshall said.

She looked over at him. "Not that anxious, actually."

He smiled at her and started to reach for her hand when headlights suddenly flashed on behind them. Marshall let out a curse as a vehicle's headlights filled their truck cab with blinding light.

"What the hell?" he said.

Alexa saw what appeared to be an old pickup riding their bumper. "Is he trying to run you off the road?"

Just then the old truck slammed into the

back of their pickup. Their truck fishtailed and the other truck fell back a little.

"Hang on," Marshall said and jammed his foot on the gas. His pickup took off down the narrow road, gravel flying.

As fast as they were going, the lights of the old pickup grew brighter and brighter behind them as the driver quickly caught up.

Alexa looked over at Marshall, then at the speedometer. They were going over a hundred. She knew there was a curve coming up. So did Marshall. She could see tension in his expression. His big hands gripped the wheel as they went down a hill and flew up another.

And suddenly the lights behind them went out. Alexa turned in her seat. The pickup was gone. It had just disappeared.

Marshall hit the brakes. The pickup skidded to a stop in the middle of the road just yards from the curve.

She could see he was shaken as he glanced back in his rearview mirror, then over at her. "Tell me that wasn't the phantom truck Dave told us about."

All Alexa could do was stare back at the empty road as her heart rate slowly dropped back to normal.

MARSHALL KNEW THERE WAS no chance in hell that he was going to be able to sleep. He stood on the porch, the August night hot and without a breath of breeze. He couldn't help thinking about the old pickup that had tried to run them off the road. That coupled with what he'd learned about the Wellingtons was bound to give him nightmares. He couldn't even imagine what it would do to Alexa tonight.

He hated dropping her off at that house, knowing what they did. He wished she would come over but when he glanced out at Wellington Manor, he saw no lights on her side of the mansion.

The night should have soothed what ailed him. He loved this time of year, loved the smells as grains ripened and grasses turned golden. Standing here, he could hear the lowing of the cattle. On nights like this, he could feel that strong connection he had with this land, this place.

Unfortunately, that old pickup that had chased them nagged at him. While he might believe evil could be passed down from generation to generation and concede that some spirits just couldn't rest, he didn't believe in phantom pickups. The truck that had tried to run them off the road had been real. He'd heard the sound of metal meeting metal. There was nothing phantom about that truck—nor its driver—and tomorrow he'd prove it.

The heat pressed down on him. He glanced toward Wellington Manor again and caught the glimmer of the pond in the dark cottonwoods. What he needed was a swim. He hadn't gone swimming in the middle of the night since he was a kid and lately he'd been feeling like a kid again.

Alexa. She was responsible for the way he was feeling. He warned himself that she would be leaving soon. She'd have to get back to her job, as she'd said. But he remembered what he'd read about her in that interview. She wanted to write children's books. Couldn't you write children's books anywhere? Even in a remote part of Montana?

He shook his head at the fantasy his thoughts had taken and, grabbing a towel, headed for the pond to cool off.

ALEXA HAD BEEN GRATEFUL TO SLIP into the house and find no one waiting up for her. She didn't know what she was going to tell her brother, but whatever she decided tomorrow would be soon enough.

She went straight to her room, unlocked the door and stepped in. Everything appeared to be as she had left it and yet she sensed that someone had been there. With all the locks the same in the house, anyone could come and go at will with a skeleton key, just as she had done.

It was late and she was exhausted after the day she'd had. She changed into a nightgown even though she doubted she would be able to sleep, her mind still whirling. What if everything that was happening was just as her brother had suspected? Something evil that emanated from this house? Some leftover evil from generations of evil?

Moving to the French doors, she stepped out on the balcony to look toward Marshall's house. His house was dark. She marveled that he was able to put everything out of his mind and go right to bed.

Alexa started to step away from the window when she saw two figures in the trees beside the house. Jayden and a young blond woman. As they slipped into the house through a back door, Alexa recognized the woman Jayden had his arm around. Sierra.

She hurriedly stepped back. Her heart threatened to break. She didn't want to believe her sister-in-law would be cheating on Landon, especially since they'd only just married. But nothing was as it should be in this house.

Angry and upset, she threw herself on the bed and closed her eyes tight against the tears. She'd come here to help her brother, and now she would be the one to break his heart. Emotionally exhausted, she fell into a deep sleep.

"Alexa?"

She stirred.

"Alexa?"

Opening her eyes, she saw her mother standing next to her bed.

"You must save your brother," her mother said. "You know what you have to do."

Startled, Alexa jerked up in the bed, blinking wildly. For a moment, she was back in her childhood bedroom. But as she blinked again the bedroom at Wellington Manor came into focus. The room was empty. Her mother was gone.

If she had ever been there at all.

But her words still hung in the air and there was a familiar smell....

Alexa bolted from the bed. Her nightgown

was drenched with sweat and she was breathing hard.

"It was just a nightmare," she whispered to herself as she stepped to the window, hoping for a breath of air.

That's when she saw him, his cowboy hat cocked back on his head. He wore nothing but jeans and boots, a towel draped over one shoulder as he sauntered toward the pond.

He disappeared behind the trees. A moment later she heard a splash.

The sound pulled her—just as the thought did of the cowboy in the cool water of the pond.

She grabbed her robe, drew it on and, taking her key, hurried out of her room. The hallway was empty. She tiptoed down the stairs and through the living room to slip out the front door.

For a moment, she stood on the step, hesitating. She'd already dragged Marshall into her nightmare. She knew what could happen if she continued down to the pond. Just the thought sent a shiver through her. She took a step, then another. As she walked through the deep shadows of the trees, she felt excitement stir within her—and desire. She began to run.

At the edge of the trees, she stopped. She

could see him swimming through the dark water, droplets washing over his brown skin, his back and shoulders shimmering in the moonlight.

She'd never seen a more beautiful man.

MARSHALL TOOK ANOTHER stroke and opened his eyes. She was standing at the edge of the trees, a vision in white. It reminded him of the first time he'd seen her.

He watched, fascinated, as she stepped from the trees, her white robe sliding off her slim sun-browned shoulders. For a moment, she stood silhouetted in the moonlight making her nightgown transparent. He could see the lush curves of her breasts, the slim waist, the full hips.

As she waded out into the water, he saw the dark of her nipples, the points hard pebbles against the fabric.

His gaze locked with hers. Slowly she reached down and lifted the hem of her nightgown, raising it up and over her head. She tossed the gown back toward the dry shore, then dove into the water and swam out toward him.

Marshall realized he had been holding his breath. She was so breathtaking. The water felt like cool silk against his skin as he took a final stroke and drifted slowly toward her.

He drew up, treading water, as she moved into him and pressed her naked body against his. Her skin felt hot and silken. Water droplets jeweled on her lashes as she looked at him—her look hotter than her skin against his. His desire spiked as he pulled her closer.

"I saw you from my window," she whispered.

"I wished on that star up there that I would find you down here," he whispered back.

They kissed, sweet, gentle kisses that grew hotter. She wrapped her legs around his waist as he deepened the kiss and treaded water to keep them afloat.

Her full breasts were pressed against his bare chest, the hard nipples tantalizing. The porcelain feel of her skin against his stole his breath, revved his heartbeat. He'd never wanted a woman the way he wanted her.

He swam them toward shore where the trees were the thickest, the spot where she'd dropped her robe.

Carrying her from the water, he laid her down on the robe, the warm earth beneath her. For a long moment, he merely stared down into her beautiful eyes. He'd never made love like this, under the moonlight, his body still cool from the water, droplets falling from his hair onto her radiant flesh.

ALEXA HAD NEVER DARED throw caution to the wind. And yet the moment she'd taken a step toward the pond—and this cowboy—she knew there would be no turning back. She'd never wanted a man enough to be so brazen until Marshall. She had opened herself up to him, but now it would be a total surrender.

He took her in his arms, his hands cradling her head as he kissed her lips, then kissed a trail of molten fire down her throat to her breasts.

Alexa sucked in a breath as his mouth captured one of her nipples. He teased it with his teeth, making her arch against him.

She reached for him, needing, wanting, pleading for him to take her. He slowly lowered himself onto her, and she felt the strength and weight of him.

She took him in, opening the last of herself to this cowboy.

MARSHALL LAY ON HIS BACK, staring up at the stars. He'd never felt such contentment. He could hear the soft lap of the pond as a fish broke the surface. In the shadows, several ducks honked softly to the flutter of wings and splashing water.

Beside him, Alexa breathed softly. He glanced over at her. She was smiling, also gazing up at the stars.

"A penny for your thoughts," he whispered.

"I've never felt like this before."

He laughed quietly and rolled onto his side to look at her. "Me either. I want to stay here forever."

She smiled ruefully. "If only we could."

A set of headlights scanned across the horizon as a vehicle pulled into Wellington Manor. Marshall and Alexa stayed hidden in the shadows of the trees down by the pond but could hear the sound of laughter and voices.

"Gigi and Devlin," Alexa said. "I hadn't realized they'd been gone when I came home."

He hadn't paid any attention to what cars were parked by the house either. He'd had too much on his mind to care.

"I should get back," she said, sitting up and reaching for her nightgown.

Marshall didn't want her to go—not back to the house, not back to Spokane. But he knew he couldn't stop her. Alexa had to finish what she'd come here to do—if she even knew what that was.

"I'm glad you came swimming with me," he whispered.

She smiled at him, touched his cheek with her cool fingers then rose to slip the nightgown over her.

He handed her the robe, now damp from where they had made love on it. She drew the fabric to her, touching it to her lips as her gaze locked with his.

"I wish I didn't have to go," she whispered.

He could only nod. There was so much he wanted to say but he sensed the timing was all wrong. "Alexa, I…I've never felt like I do right now."

She kissed him. He pulled her closer for a moment, her kiss lingering on his lips. "I'll see you tomorrow."

And then she was gone, a white vision disappearing into the trees as she hurried toward Wellington Manor.

Marshall had the impulse to go after her, fear growing inside him that he wouldn't see her again because that house and the people in it would be the death of her.

ALEXA SLIPPED IN THROUGH THE front door and padded barefoot past the dark kitchen. Gigi and Devlin must have already gone upstairs. She breathed a sigh of relief as she headed for the stairs and froze as a door opened down the hall.

Sierra came out of Jayden's room and started toward her. Still cloaked in shadow, Alexa quickly stepped into an alcove beneath the stairs an instant before Sierra passed. She was dressed in her nightgown and robe, barefoot, her hair a mess.

Alexa wanted to confront her. But instead, she pressed her back against the wall as Sierra hurried up the stairs.

For a long time, Alexa stood, shaking inside. A part of her regretted not approaching her sister-in-law right there and then. But she knew that Sierra would turn this around somehow and the person who would suffer the most would be Landon.

It was going to break Landon's heart when she told him. But what was the alternative? Wait and let him find out on his own? Or have an accident that left Sierra a rich widow?

So Alexa stood there in the dark, giving Sierra enough time to return to her room. Her earlier contentment gone, she finally padded up the stairs. Alexa was almost to the top when she saw Jayden standing in the hall, watching her.

She didn't know how long he'd been there, but there was no doubt he knew she'd seen Sierra coming out of his room and he didn't look happy about it.

Chapter Eleven

Marshall awoke thinking about the pickup that had chased them and tried to run them off the road the night before. At breakfast at the ranch, he mentioned he'd seen the phantom truck.

His brothers laughed, but he asked anyway, "Logan, you said some friends of yours had been chased by it. When was that?"

"Probably fifteen years ago now."

"Did they describe the truck?" Marshall asked.

"You aren't serious, right?" Zane said.

"An old-model Chevy, stepside, two-toned. Is that what chased you?" Logan asked.

Marshall nodded as he rose from the table.

"I wouldn't go messing with somethin' you don't know about," Logan warned.

"That's just it. I think I do know what I'm messing with," Marshall said. "The question now is only who's behind it?"

After leaving the ranch, he drove up the same road he and Alexa had taken the night before. He slowed at the point where he'd first seen the pickup appear behind him and turned his pickup around in the middle of the road to drive back over a small rise.

At the bottom were tracks in the dirt that led back into a stand of trees. From the trees, someone could have seen him and Alexa coming up the road, waited until they passed then pulled out and followed with their headlights off until they topped the rise and seemed to appear out of nowhere.

He drove to the point where the pickup had seemingly vanished. This time he knew what to look for and found where the pickup had left the road. The driver had done his best to cover the tracks, but Marshall was still able to follow them back into a stand of Russian olive trees around an old dump.

The pickup was hidden among a half-dozen other old vehicles that had been abandoned there. Most of the others were older. Stopping the truck, Marshall climbed out, wary of rattlesnakes in all this junk.

The phantom pickup was a 1956 Chevy 3100 stepside pickup, its two-toned paint long faded. As he opened the driver's side door, he saw that mice had nested in the floorboards and bench seat. But someone had brushed the nests from behind the steering wheel last night.

As he slid in, he made a note of how far back the seat had been pushed. The driver had been long legged, probably male. The other time the phantom truck had made its run had been because some teenagers had been snooping around Wellington Manor. Marshall didn't believe it was any coincidence that the driver of the truck had come after Alexa and him last night. Someone at that house knew she'd been snooping around. And probably suspected he was helping her.

As he climbed out of the old pickup, he wondered which of the males at the house had been driving this truck last night. There were four men at the house: Archer, Devlin, Jayden and Landon.

Marshall started to correct himself, to leave Alexa's brother off his suspect list, but unlike Alexa he didn't trust any of them—Landon included.

Someone had tried to scare them last night. Which meant that someone feared Alexa was getting too close to whatever secret they were trying to keep in that house.

FROM WORKING IN JOURNALISM, Alexa had made a lot of contacts over the years. It took only a few calls on her cell phone to get what she needed the next morning. She'd driven into Whitehorse and used her cell phone, afraid to talk on the Wellington Manor phone for fear someone would be listening on another line.

"I have the obit and the police report right here," a young journalist in Nevada told her.

"Police report?" Alexa said, glancing out the SUV window as a car went by. She couldn't help feeling paranoid, given everything that had happened.

"The suicide was investigated as a possible homicide," the reporter said. "The father, J. A. Wellington, died of a fatal gunshot wound to the head in their home outside of Las Vegas. He'd been a financial consultant. Turned out it was all a scam. He'd bilked investors out of millions of dollars."

"Does it mention the wife and daughter?" she asked.

"The wife was cleared. Apparently she knew nothing about her husband's business and wasn't home at the time of the murder."

"What happened to them?" Alexa asked, thinking of a recent case like this where the family was left penniless.

"The wife and daughter left the state. We did a follow-up story five years later when the daughter was sixteen. The two were living down near Los Angeles in some dump. The wife was working as a waitress, but they were barely getting by. It was pretty sad. Apparently the husband knew the feds were on to him and killed himself. But what made the case interesting is that the money was never recovered."

At the age of eleven, Sierra Wellington had gone from filthy rich to flat broke. Alexa could only assume what that had done to Sierra.

Alexa felt her heart begin to pound. Was it possible she was secretly looking for the money in the house while pretending to remodel it for a bed-and-breakfast? "How is it possible that the money he stole never turned up?"

"Maybe he socked it away in another country or turned it into gold bars and buried it. Who knows?"

"But if that was the case, then why would he kill himself and not tell anyone where it was?" Alexa asked, thinking out loud.

"Maybe he *did* tell someone," the reporter

said. "But it wasn't the wife. The feds kept an eye on her. She died broke."

"What about the daughter?" Alexa asked, wondering if the feds were keeping an eye on her or if they thought she was too young at the time of her father's death to know anything about it.

"Last I heard she was in college on a hardship-case scholarship."

MARSHALL WAS GLAD TO get Alexa's call. He'd tried the house and was told that she must have gone into town as her SUV was missing.

He could hear what sounded like arguing in the background and had barely hung up when Alexa had called. Marshall listened as she filled him in on what she'd found out about her sister-in-law.

"You think her father told Sierra where he hid the money?"

"Maybe. Maybe not," Alexa said. "But I wouldn't be surprised if she thinks it's in that house. It would explain a lot."

He agreed. "But wasn't it the old-maid relative who left her the house, not her father?"

"I'm not sure anyone left her the house. From what I've been able to find out, the house was tied up in the niece's estate. Sierra had petitioned for it as the last living Wellington and finally got the mansion. Apparently she'd been trying to get it for some time."

"It certainly sounds like she was anxious to have it," Marshall said. "But if she knew where the money was hidden, wouldn't she have already found it?"

"Maybe he didn't tell her where. Sierra told me that the woman closed off most of the house, living only on the first floor in the servants' quarters. So if Sierra's father paid the niece a visit and hid the money, thinking he was going to get away with all of it, it could be anywhere. You could hide millions of dollars in that house and it might never be found."

"Still it seems crazy for her father to kill himself after all he went through to steal the money, and then not tell anyone where he hid it," Marshall said. "Sierra was eleven at the time, right? Maybe he didn't tell her for fear she couldn't keep the secret."

"Maybe," Alexa replied.

When she said no more, he told her about the pickup he'd found hidden at the old dump. "Someone was trying to scare us off. They don't like you snooping around. I'm worried what they will do next."

"So far all they've done is try to scare me," Alexa said. "I just hate that I've dragged you into this."

As if she could keep him out, he thought, and said as much. "I hope you don't regret last night."

Her laugh filled him with pleasure. "I could never regret last night."

"Me either. Listen, there's been some trouble at the ranch. I have to go by there and make sure my stepmother is all right. Call me later?"

"The group at the house were talking about going into town tonight to listen to some country-western band. Even Carolina has agreed to go along. I'm not sure if she has changed her mind about leaving here or if she just needs to get out of this house for a while since she can't seem to get a flight out yet," Alexa said. "If they do, I plan to see what they've been working on in this house."

"Count me in. Just promise me you won't do it alone."

She laughed again. "I'm brave, but not that brave. The truth is this place gives me the creeps."

Marshall figured it was a lot more than that. If there was even a chance that Alexa

had her mother's gift, then she had to be terrified of what she might see in that house.

ALEXA THOUGHT ABOUT WHAT Marshall had
said. She was convinced that Sierra's father
could have told the girl about the money. If
he knew his daughter, he wouldn't have been
worried about her being able to keep a secret.
Sierra, Alexa believed, was like her father.
She wouldn't have talked for fear someone
might take the money from her or she might
have to share it.

It was that last thought that sent an icy
dagger straight to her heart. She had just assumed that Sierra had married Landon for his
money, which still might be true.

But if she found the millions, she wouldn't
need him anymore—and from the little Alexa
had seen of Sierra, she knew the woman
wouldn't want to share. Not that Landon
would let Sierra keep the money if he knew
where it had come from.

She was even more worried about her
brother but dreaded telling him everything
she'd learned. The truth was, she feared he
wouldn't believe her. So far, all she had was
conjecture. Nothing she learned proved that

his life was in danger. Or even that Sierra was having an affair with Jayden.

But if she could find where someone in this house had been searching for the missing millions...

First though, she had to find out everything she could about the people now staying in that house. At the county library, Alexa got on the internet and began her search. There wasn't a lot to find on the occupants of Wellington Manor because they were young and hadn't done much with their lives yet.

But thanks to the internet, she was able to gather what was there easily. She started with the men. Devlin Landers had been the star of his debate team in high school and in college had majored in prelaw. He had married Gigi Brown after graduation. Gigi had been the head cheerleader in high school and a mediocre student in college, who'd majored in art history.

Archer Durand had been a football star in high school, played a little in college until he was injured then seemed to be more interested in the social life at his frat house. He'd majored in mass communication and had married Carolina Bates his senior year, her junior year.

Alexa frowned. Why did that name sound so familiar? She shook her head and typed in Carolina Bates. She had been a good student, graduating at the top of her class and had gone to college on a scholarship, majoring in criminal law.

She typed in Jayden Farrell. A half-dozen names came up, none of them matching the one staying at Wellington Manor. As far as she could tell, Jayden Farrell didn't exist—or he'd lied about who he was.

It struck her that Sierra might not be the only person looking for the millions her father had stolen.

By the time Alexa reached the house, the driveway was empty. She opened the door and called out, "Anyone here?"

No answer. But just to be safe, she walked down to Jayden's room and knocked. When there was no answer, she tried the knob. Locked. Using her key, she opened his door.

The room was almost too neat. He'd apparently brought little with him to Montana. She did a quick search, then, feeling the hair stand on the back of her neck, she spun around, half expecting to find him standing behind her.

There was no one there, but it had spooked

her enough that she left his room and w
to the phone.

"They've all gone into town," she said
when Marshall answered. "Want to come
over and see if we're right about what they've
been doing over here?"

"I'll be right over."

True to his word, Marshall cut across the
pasture and was there minutes later. She
quickly filled him in on what she'd learned
during her internet search.

"Jayden caught me coming home the other
night. I'd left a light on and he'd turned it out
and waited for me."

"You think he was trying to scare you?"

"Actually, I got the feeling he was trying to
warn me. If anyone knows what's going on
in this house, it's Jayden. And when I tried to
find out more about him, I came up blank. I
think he lied about who he is. I'm wondering
how many people are looking for the money
in this house?"

"They all could be working together," Marshall said.

Alexa didn't want to believe that, since it
would be harder for Landon not to be a part of
it and she refused to think he knew anything
about what was going on.

She led the way upstairs, and using the skeleton key from her room, began opening doors along the second floor. In each of the rooms, they could see places in the plaster-and-lath walls had been repaired.

"Are you thinking what I am?" Marshall asked.

"Someone has been looking in the walls, then repairing them when they haven't found what they were looking for?"

He nodded.

They found the same types of patch jobs in all the rooms and along the hallway. On the third floor, they wandered through the furniture and boxes. Everywhere behind them were places where someone had been searching, no doubt for the millions J. A. Wellington had stolen.

"It looks like they have run out of places to search," Marshall said after they'd found more patch jobs throughout the first floor as well.

"Except for the basement."

The door to the basement, they found, was padlocked. Marshall shot her a look. "Why would they padlock this door but no others?"

"Because they haven't finished searching down there. Can you open it?"

"Not without someone knowing we did."

She didn't care. "Open it."

From the tool bucket he found in a corner in the kitchen, he pulled out a hacksaw and went to work on the lock. A few moments later, she heard the lock snap open.

The door swung in to expose a dark stairway to an even darker basement.

Marshall handed her one of the flashlights he'd taken from the tool bucket, then pulled out the one he'd brought from home before leading the way down the stairs.

"I HAD TO MEET AGGIE AND put an end to this," Emma said, tired of all the questions and recriminations. "I made a decision. Maybe it was wrong—"

"Maybe?" Hoyt snapped. He had taken off his Stetson and now raked both hands through his hair in exasperation. Across the kitchen table, Sheriff McCall Crawford looked just as upset.

"I had to see what Aggie had found," Emma said as she motioned to the contents of the envelope that had been dumped out on her kitchen table.

"I saw your expression when you looked at the photographs," she said to her husband.

"There's a chance the woman Aggie found is Laura, isn't there?"

He glared at her from across the table.

"You should have told me about the note and your plan to meet Aggie," the sheriff said.

"Aggie couldn't bring this to you," Emma replied to McCall. "She was afraid you wouldn't listen to her."

"What was the plan after she gave you this information?" McCall asked.

Emma made a point of not looking at her husband as she said, "Aggie and I were going to confront her."

Hoyt made a furious sound, shoved himself to his feet and walked out of the room for a few moments.

"Aggie was afraid that if this woman—"

"Sharon Jones."

"Right, if she thought law enforcement was on to her, she would disappear and then Aggie couldn't prove that she wasn't crazy—and I wouldn't know when Laura was going to strike."

"Laura is dead," Hoyt snapped as he came back into the room.

Emma shot him a look. "Is she? Can you definitely say that this woman is not Laura?"

"Yes. Because I saw her drown."

"You said the boating trip was Laura's idea," Emma said patiently. "Why would a woman who allegedly hated water and couldn't swim well want to go on a boat trip on Fort Peck Reservoir, especially when she was planning to divorce you?"

"I have no idea but she did."

"Exactly. And you said yourself that she was horribly jealous. If you even looked at another woman—"

"Emma," he said, dropping down in front of her and taking her hands in his. "Honey, you have to stop this. You are getting as nuts as that damned insurance investigator."

The memory of Aggie's cry after the shot was fired and her fall into the river sent a stab of pain through Emma.

"I believe Aggie." She looked to the sheriff. "Have your deputies found her yet?"

McCall shook her head. "We're dragging the river now."

Emma nodded, wondering if they would find her body. Laura Chisholm's body had never been found in Fort Peck Reservoir.

"What about Sharon Jones?" she asked the sheriff.

"I've contacted the Billings police. They're going to pick her up for questioning."

"Can you get DNA or fingerprints or something to prove who she is?" Emma asked.

"We'll take it one step at a time once she is picked up," McCall said.

Emma nodded, hoping Aggie wasn't right about what would happen.

THE BASEMENT DOOR OPENED on a room with a low ceiling crisscrossed with plumbing pipes.

Marshall shone the flashlight beam around the room, found a switch and several overhead bulbs blinked on.

The basement smelled musty and damp. Alexa hugged herself, trying to ignore the cold as well as whatever else had been down here. Impressions of dark events rushed over her. She closed her eyes for a moment, fighting off the house's past.

"Are you all right?" Marshall asked.

She nodded and opened her eyes.

"You don't have to do this."

"Yes, I do."

He gave her an encouraging smile. "Then let's see what's here."

As he shone the flashlight down one corridor after another, it reminded her of a subway tunnel. The chill, the smells, the clank of the old pipes.

"Which way?" Marshall asked.

"Look at the floor," Alexa said, after remembering the third floor and the trail through the dust. It wasn't as dusty down here, but there were scuff marks on the concrete—and mud. They followed them down one of the corridors.

Alexa had never been claustrophobic—until now. The low-hanging, large, corroded pipes seemed to press down on her. The basement was a maze of narrow aisles that ran between whatever machinery had originally provided heat and possibly electricity to the mansion. She found herself ducking her head even though, as tall as Marshall was, he didn't need to duck.

The trail ended in a dead end. Alexa knelt down to pick up a piece of dried mud from a boot sole. It had been dropped just inches from where the wall ended.

"This wall isn't concrete like the others," Marshall noted.

"There's a way through here," she said and began to search for a panel or switch that would open the wall.

Marshall found it, a small handle that looked as if it turned off water to the plumbing overhead. Instead, when he pulled it, a panel slid back into the wall with a groan.

He shot her a look as he shone his flashlight beam into the darkness beyond the wall.

Alexa saw another long corridor, this a tunnel, narrow and cramped. The smell coming out of it turned her stomach. The last place she wanted to go was down there.

"Why don't you stay here," Marshall suggested, no doubt seeing her revulsion.

It was tempting. But the option was waiting here for him. "Let's go," she said, happy to let him lead the way.

Marshall blocked the door open with an old, heavy gear wheel he found in the corner and they started down the tunnel.

Alexa could hear what sounded like mice scurrying ahead of them. But it was what else she felt that had her trembling. Something horrible had happened down here. Her skin crawled, rippling with gooseflesh, as she fought to keep out the images that flashed inside her head.

They hadn't gone far when they came to something that brought Marshall up short. She heard him let out a curse, then turn to try to shield her from it.

But she'd already felt the horror and leaned

past him to look. Even knowing what it was, she hadn't been prepared for the cage.

It had been built back into the earth like a root cellar, only this small hole had been fitted with bars to keep something inside.

Or someone. She shuddered and turned away. Marshall put his arm around her and pulled her into his chest. Like her, he must be thinking about the great-great-grandmother who'd gone crazy after the death of her daughter and granddaughter. Dave had said the basement was where the granddaughter's body had been found.

"It was the screaming," Alexa said. "He put her down here so he didn't have to hear it." She felt Marshall shudder, but he didn't pull away. Instead he drew her closer, smoothing her hair with his hand. "Have you seen enough?"

She shook her head. "We have to know what is at the end of this tunnel. If they've found the money."

"I would imagine that if they had, they would be long gone," Marshall said.

Maybe. Or maybe they would hide the money again until they could leave without causing any suspicion, Alex thought, thinking of Jayden, who'd already announced he would be leaving soon now that summer was almost over.

Marshall let go of her to shine the flashlight beam down the tunnel. The mud trail continued into the darkness ahead, the tunnel growing narrower, the air colder and danker.

Alexa saw him glance at his watch. They had to move quickly now. Time was running out. She didn't dare think about what could happen if they were caught down here.

Chapter Twelve

Marshall led the way as the tunnel grew more cramped. He'd never minded small places but this tunnel gave him the creeps. He kept seeing that cage back there in the wall. Alexa had known what it was for. He didn't even want to consider how she'd known.

Whatever was going on in this house, someone wanted to keep it a secret. Bad enough to kill?

He didn't want to find out.

Alexa was scared. He could see it in her face, but as he'd learned about her, she was strong and determined. That strength wouldn't let her turn back. Not yet.

"Let's move a little faster," he said, not wanting to alarm her and yet at the same time growing more anxious with each step.

They moved quickly down the tunnel until they reached a spot where someone had been digging in the wall. Bricks had been removed and stacked to one side. The hole was large—and empty.

"Is it a large enough hole to hold millions of dollars?" Alexa asked as her flashlight beam bore into the empty space.

"Depends on what he'd put the money in before he hid it," Marshall said and noted other holes in the brick walls. "It's hard to say if they found something of interest or not."

"But was it the same person who's been searching the rest of the house? Or someone else?" Alexa sighed. "I wonder what they did with the loot if they found it?"

"Squirreled it away somewhere until they can make their exit."

She nodded. "Let's get out of here."

Marshall shone his flashlight to where the tunnel ended just yards away in a set of stairs. "An exit?"

Stepping to the stairs, he looked up at what appeared to be a door. He shot Alexa a look, then tried the handle.

THE DOOR OPENED ONTO another set of stairs. Alexa could smell fresh air and bolted up the steps, but quickly stopped when she saw that the exit was covered with what appeared to be a heavy wooden gate.

"Let me," Marshall said, stepping past her. He handed her his flashlight and pushed on the gate. She'd expected it to be heavy, but the gate swung open with relative ease, exposing starlight in the dark canopy overhead and the feathery dark leaves of a cottonwood branch etched against the night sky.

She smelled the water at the pond even before she saw the moonlight glimmering off the smooth surface.

"It's a secret way in and out of the house," she said, stating the obvious. Is this how the lovers she'd seen the first time had been coming and going?

The gate was hidden behind some large rocks and bushes. She wondered who knew about this.

"We should retrace our steps and cover our tracks as best we can," Marshall said. But even as he spoke, Alexa saw car lights top the nearby hill and head this way.

"It's too late," she said. "We can't possibly get back before they enter the house and there is only one way up out of the basement—at least that we know of. They're going to find the broken padlock anyway."

Marshall let out a curse under his breath.

"It's one thing for them to know that you were down in the basement. I left the tunnel open."

"It doesn't matter," Alexa said as the cars turned into the drive, the headlights sweeping toward them. "It's time I tell my brother everything."

They ducked down behind the rocks and bushes as the two vehicles came down the lane, stopping in front of the mansion.

They stayed like that until the others had gone inside.

"What if your brother already knows?"

She shot Marshall a shocked look.

"I don't want to upset you, but what if he got you here not to chase away the ghosts, but use your…instincts to tell him where the money was hidden? Or who already found it."

Alexa couldn't help her anger or her disappointment. "You don't know my brother."

"No, I don't. But I hate to see you get hurt. I'm afraid of what will happen when you tell him what you know."

Alexa walked up through the trees from the pond, taking her time in case she was being watched from one of the many windows.

She was furious with Marshall for even suggesting that her brother could be after the stolen money and even more furious with herself because she hadn't gone to her brother with the truth sooner.

Her excuse had been that she hated the thought of breaking her brother's heart. But the truth was, she was afraid. Afraid of his reaction. She feared Sierra might be right. If push came to shove, Landon would side with his wife—no matter how much evidence there was against Sierra.

Cursing her own doubts about her brother, she still feared for his safety. Whoever had found the money might decide to step up his or her timeline. If Sierra was involved, Alexa feared that the ultimate plan was to get rid of Landon—and her as well, now that she'd become embroiled in this.

What if she couldn't convince her brother to leave this house—and Sierra?

As she opened the front door, Gigi turned from the fire. Archer was throwing more wood on the blaze, the two of them complaining about the cold Montana summer night.

Just then, Devlin came out of the kitchen, carrying a tray with a bottle of wine and a half-dozen glasses.

"Oh, good, there you are," Landon said, appearing right behind her. "We were just about to have a nightcap. I was hoping you would join us."

Alexa felt her stomach knot. After being drugged once she wasn't about to consume anything in this house that she didn't see someone else drink first.

She looked into her brother's face. This was the most relaxed she'd seen him since she arrived. She felt herself weaken. No way did Landon know what was going on in this house. And yet how could he not suspect?

As she let her gaze travel around the living room, her eyes rested on Jayden. Who better than to sneak down to the basement at night than the single man? The man who insisted on staying in the servants' quarters of the house on the main floor instead of in one of the grander rooms upstairs.

Her heart began to pound. What about the woman he'd met down by the pond? She suspected they had used the tunnel exit to meet. So at least one other person in this house had to know about the digging in the tunnel walls. Sierra? Or one of the other women?

"Join us," Sierra said. She appeared to have already had more than a little something to drink.

Alexa had no choice. "Thank you," she said

as she watched Devlin pour the wine. Alexa took the glass she was offered, but simply held it between her hands as she moved over to the fire.

As she pretended to study the wine in the firelight, she secretly watched each of the people in the room, waiting for someone to take the first drink of the wine.

"None for me," Jayden said as Devlin tried to hand him a glass.

Alexa noticed that Devlin didn't take any either.

"To the future," Landon said, coming over to the fire to join Alexa. He lightly touched his wine glass to hers and raised his to his lips, stopping when she didn't do the same.

"Is something wrong?" he asked.

"No." She smiled, her heart hammering in her chest. How could she suspect her brother of anything, let alone drugging her? She raised her glass to her lips.

The glass slipped from her fingers, crashed on the fireplace hearth and shattered, sending red wine into the air to land like blood splatters on the floor.

Sierra let out a cry. "My great-great-grandmother's crystal!"

"I'm so sorry," Alexa said as she quickly

hurried into the kitchen to get something to clean up the mess.

"It's no big deal," Landon said to her retreating back.

"What do you mean, 'no big deal'?" Sierra demanded. "Do you have any idea how much that glass was worth?"

"I'll buy you one that costs twice as much," Landon snapped.

The living room fell into a heavy, tense silence.

"I'm going to call it a night," Jayden said. The others agreed.

By the time Alexa returned to the living room, only Landon and Sierra remained. Landon had picked up the larger pieces of glass.

Sierra was standing with her back to the room, and from the way she was standing, she was clearly still furious. "You really know how to ruin a party," she said to Alexa.

"Sierra," Landon hissed under his breath.

"Well, she does."

"It was an accident," Landon said. "There is no harm done."

Sierra pouted but said nothing as Alexa and Landon cleaned up the mess.

"I'll be happy to replace the glass," Alexa said to her sister-in-law.

"That isn't necessary," Landon said.

"It wouldn't be the same anyway," Sierra said.

"I suggest you not use the glasses if they mean that much to you," Landon said through gritted teeth. "I'm going to bed. Can I see you up?" he asked his sister.

Sierra started to protest but Landon cut her off. "I haven't had hardly any time with my sister."

"That's because we are all trying to get this house ready for paying guests," Sierra snapped. "Not to mention your sister has been spending all her time with that cowboy."

Landon shot his wife a look that made her clamp her lips shut, then he and Alexa turned and left.

As they started up the stairs, Alexa looked back. Sierra hadn't touched her wine. The others had left their glasses untouched on the coffee table. She and Landon were almost to the top of the stairs when they heard a crash. Alexa looked back to see that Sierra had thrown the nearly empty wine bottle against the stone fireplace.

Landon's jaw tightened, but he didn't look back.

"I KNOW WHAT YOU'RE GOING to say," Landon said once they were in Alexa's room, the door closed.

A light breeze played at the curtains at the open French doors, the air cool, stars glittering in the huge velvet sky.

Alexa hadn't realized how late it was. Her eyelids felt like sandpaper and she felt tired all over. "I doubt that," she said and plopped down onto the loveseat, too exhausted to stand any longer.

"Sierra is young and headstrong and…" He met his sister's gaze. "Spoiled."

Alexa kept silent. Her brother was intelligent. He had to see that it was more than that.

"What is it you want me to say?" she asked finally.

He chuckled. "Tell me I didn't make a mistake."

She looked up at him and sadly shook her head. "I love you so much."

"I know."

"I just want you to be happy."

"I know," he said as he lowered himself to the chair opposite the loveseat. "I realize now I had a lot of reasons for inviting you here, all of them selfish."

"You were right. There is something going on in this house," Alexa said. "But it isn't the spirits you're worried about, is it?"

"Sometimes I wake up in the middle of the night and Sierra is gone from our bed," he said slowly. "When I ask her about it, she says she has trouble sleeping and likes wandering through the house at night because it's quiet."

"Do you believe her?" Alexa asked.

"I want to." He rubbed the back of his neck, looking as exhausted as she felt. "I haven't wanted to tell Sierra, but I don't want to run a bed-and-breakfast."

It surprised Alexa that he was finally being honest with her. "Why haven't you told her?"

He shook his head. "She seems so set on this.... I don't want to break her heart."

Too bad Sierra didn't feel the same way about him. "You're afraid if it came down to an ultimatum, she would choose the house."

He nodded, then let out a humorless laugh. "Says a lot about my faith in my wife."

"Says more about her feelings for..." Alexa was going to say "you." But quickly changed it to "this house."

"It's all she has," Landon said. "She's never had anything that she can call her own since she was a girl."

"She has you."

He smiled at that.

"Has she talked to you about her past? Her father?"

"I know he killed himself."

"Did you know that he also bilked a lot of money out of his investors?" She saw her brother start to defend the man. "The feds were about to arrest him when he killed himself."

Landon sighed and sank back into his chair. "That explains a lot, huh."

"The money was never recovered."

He looked up in surprise and she nodded.

"I believe he hid it in this house, and I'm not the only one who believes that. Someone has been looking for it. I think they might have found it."

Landon stared at her. "Sierra?"

"Maybe. It's millions of dollars. Are you sure she ever really planned to open a bed-and-breakfast? Or was it just a way to look for the money without anyone suspecting?"

He shook his head. "If Sierra found the money, why wouldn't she..." His voice trailed off as he realized why his wife wouldn't have told him. "What am I going to do, Alexa?"

"I can't tell you what to do, but I think you need to talk to her, tell her how you feel." She almost added, "Find out where she really goes at night," but bit her tongue. "You need to resolve this. Once you're honest with her, maybe she'll be honest with you and you'll know what to do."

He rose to his feet to leave.

"But Landon, be careful. I'm worried about these accidents you've been having."

A sadness washed over his features. "I wondered if she'd married me for my money. Yes, sis, it did cross my mind. But if she now has millions…"

"Or someone else in this house does." She could see he hadn't thought of that.

"You be careful too," he said, suddenly looking worried.

"We both need to get out of here," Alexa said. "Maybe we should go—" She was going to say "tonight" but he cut her off with a shake of his head.

"Tomorrow."

She couldn't hide her relief. "Tomorrow." As he left, she prayed tomorrow would be soon enough.

MARSHALL MENTALLY KICKED himself all the way back to his house. He shouldn't have accused Alexa's brother, knowing how protective she was of him.

He went over their last words to each other

with every step he took on the way across the pasture toward home.

"You're that sure he isn't involved in whatever this is?" he'd asked. He could see that she hadn't wanted to believe it, but she had a blind side to her when it came to her brother.

"Why would he get me here if that was true?"

He had hated to ask, but he'd felt he had to. "You say your brother inherited a lot of money. I assume you did too." He took her silence for a yes. "Who inherits if you die?"

He had seen the fear that leaped to her eyes for just an instant.

"My brother wouldn't—"

"But his wife would?"

She had looked at him, opened her mouth and closed it again then left him standing there as she headed back to that damned house.

He'd wanted to go after her, drag her into his arms and kiss some sense into her. But he'd known how well that would have gone over. He wanted desperately to keep her safe, but one of the reasons he loved her was that she never took the easy way out.

Loved her. The thought made him stumble and almost fall just yards from his house.

He swore. He'd always considered himself

a reasonable man. Falling in love at the bat of an eye wasn't reasonable. Falling in love with a total stranger... Maybe worse, a woman whom he knew saw things he never wanted to know about.

He shook his head. As much as he wanted to deny it, he'd fallen in love with that woman.

Turning, he looked back at the house and knew he was no longer a reasonable man. He'd fallen in love with this woman in the bat of an eye and it scared the hell out of him.

The question now was, what was he going to do about it?

ALEXA JUST WANTED TO FALL into the bed and sleep until noon. Tomorrow she would pack and leave—as soon as she was sure Landon was leaving as well.

But tonight, she just wanted to close her eyes in dreamless sleep.

Unfortunately, her mind had something else to say about that. She kept thinking of the tunnel, the cage, the missing bricks where someone had been looking for something— and Marshall.

She hated that she'd left things so badly with him. She hated worse admitting that what he'd said had scared her, because she'd feared he might be right. She'd seen how Landon was around Sierra. How he had overlooked whatever his wife had been up to in the middle of the night. And how he hadn't told his wife how he really felt about this house's future.

Not that Alexa believed for a moment that Sierra had any intention of making Wellington Manor a bed-and-breakfast. All of Sierra's love for this house was nothing more than a ruse. Once she retrieved her father's stolen money, she would be out of here in a heartbeat. Not even her great-great-grandmother's crystal could keep that girl in this house. Again.

Unable to sleep, Alexa got up, pulled on her robe and opened her bedroom door. The hallway was empty. There wasn't a sound other than the sounds old houses always made.

Taking her key, she locked her room, thinking how foolish that was, given that anyone with a skeleton key could get in any room in this house.

Pocketing her key, she headed downstairs to the kitchen. She needed something to help her sleep. No milk and cookies, thank you.

In the kitchen, she found a loaf of half-eaten bread, cut herself a slice then found peanut butter, her favorite, and huckleberry jam. She made herself a peanut-butter sandwich and washed it down with a glass of orange juice from the fridge.

Tomorrow she would apologize to Marshall. That and the sandwich made her feel better. Alexa thought that she might be able to sleep now. As she quietly left the kitchen and started for the stairs, she looked down the hallway to the servants' quarters—and saw Sierra coming out of Jayden's room.

Just then the old clock on the mantel struck two in the morning, making her jump. She ducked back under the stairs, plastering herself against the wall.

She could hear Sierra coming down the hallway. She prayed that her sister-in-law would go up the stairs, but of course Sierra would do just the opposite.

Sierra walked right past her and into the kitchen. Alexa let out the breath she'd been holding as she heard her sister-in-law getting something from the refrigerator.

Curious where Sierra was headed next, Alexa moved into the space under the stairs so she was better hidden.

A few minutes later, Sierra came out of the kitchen with two bottles of beer. She padded back down the hallway. At Jayden's door, she didn't knock but simply opened it and, glancing back toward the living room, stepped inside and closed the door after her.

Alexa felt sick to her stomach. She knew Sierra must have been the woman she saw with Jayden, first arguing, then in his arms. She'd seen her coming out of his room the other time, Sierra's hair a mess, in her robe. How much more evidence did she need?

Landon needed to know the truth. It would make it much easier for him to leave Sierra, to leave this house.

But as much as Alexa wanted her brother away from Sierra and this house, she couldn't bring herself to tell him tonight. She suspected he now realized that Sierra had probably been lying to him about a lot of things. Alexa had to let him handle this his own way.

So why didn't he go looking for his wife on those nights when he woke to find her gone? Because he knew what he'd discover and he wasn't ready to face it yet.

Alexa waited until she was sure Sierra wouldn't be coming back out of Jayden's room, before hurrying back up the stairs to her room.

She unlocked the door, stepped in and

locked the door behind her. For a moment she merely studied the room. It didn't appear anyone had been in here since she'd left.

Walking over to the bureau against the wall, she moved to the end of it and then, putting her weight into it, shoved the bureau across the floor.

She didn't care about the noise it made, figuring no one would hear anyway, given that everyone was in their own wings.

Once she had it blocking the door, she stripped off her robe and tumbled into the bed. She fell into a deep sleep—until she was awakened by her greatest fear. Her mother was standing by her bed.

ALEXA WOKE WITH A START, half expecting to see her mother standing beside her bed. It had been just a dream, she told herself, and yet she shuddered at the memory as she looked around the room and realized it was still dark outside. Glancing at the clock, she saw that she'd only been asleep for less than an hour.

But something had brought her out of a deep sleep so abruptly that she found herself sitting up in the bed, her heart pounding. The nightmare? No.

A name.

She blinked. Bates. She remembered why it had seemed so familiar. It was one of the two names she'd seen on the burned papers she'd retrieved from Sierra's fireplace.

At the time, the papers had appeared to be financial documents. But that hadn't meant anything to Alexa because she hadn't known about J. A. Wellington bilking all those investors out of their money.

One of those investors had been named Bates.

She grabbed for her phone, found the number of the reporter she'd spoken with and quickly called him.

After apologizing for the early hour, she said, "I need to know if there is a Bates on the list of investors that Wellington cheated."

"Just a minute." He came back on the line a few moments later. "Bates. Yep. Harold and Carol Bates."

Carolina's parents, she recalled from Carolina's wedding announcement. The father had been deceased.

Alexa's heart pounded. "Can you tell me if any of these names are on the list?" She read off the names of the other occupants of the house.

"Sorry."

She frowned, remembering the other name on the burned sheet of paper from the fire. "What about a Welch?"

"I don't see a Welch."

She wasn't sure whether she should be relieved or not that none of the other people in the house appeared to have ties to J. A. Wellington. "There isn't a Farrell?"

"Nope." He'd already told her, but she'd had to ask again.

"Isn't it possible J. A. spent all the money?"

He laughed. "Trust me, he didn't spend it or the feds would have known."

She thought of Carolina's parents. "These people who lost their money were already wealthy, right?"

"Nope. They were middle-class and lower-income people who couldn't afford to lose their life's savings. He destroyed a lot of families."

"If that is true, how was he able to accumulate millions?"

"Apparently he was good at investing their money, showing them large enough returns to keep them from withdrawing their funds. Look, I don't know where you're going with this, but if there is a story here…"

"Don't worry, I'll make sure you get it," she said, thanked him and hung up.

She had to see Carolina. The only way to put a stop to all this was to expose what was going on. It was too much of a coincidence that Carolina just happened to be the daughter of parents who had been cheated by Wellington.

Carolina either suspected the ill-gotten money was here or thought Sierra's interest in the house meant she knew where her father had hidden it.

The question was, did Sierra know that Carolina's family was one of the ones bilked by her father? Las Vegas was large enough that Sierra might not have known Carolina.

It explained what Carolina was doing here, but what if she wasn't the only one in the house after the money? What about her husband, Gigi and Devlin, and Jayden? And why, if Sierra was after the money for herself, had she invited these people to the house?

Alexa realized that Carolina might be after more than the money—she could be set on revenge.

She quickly dressed, desperately needing to talk to Carolina. But as she started down the hall, she heard voices downstairs. The moment she walked into the kitchen, she realized something had happened. Everyone but Carolina was sitting around the table with long faces.

"What's going on?" she asked and thought for a moment they weren't going to tell her.

"Carolina and Archer had another fight," Landon said. "Carolina's catching a ride to Billings today instead of waiting for a flight out."

She saw then that Archer was dabbing at his bleeding nose with a napkin. "The bitch hit me."

"Don't talk about Carolina like that," Gigi snapped. "She's upset."

"*I'm* upset," Archer snapped back. His face was also scratched. "But I'm sick of her acting like I'm a big disappointment to her."

"Where is she?" Alexa asked.

"Up in our room, but I wouldn't go up there if I were you," Archer said. "She said she wanted to be left alone."

Alexa just bet she did. Carolina had found the perfect way to make her exit with the money and without anyone suspecting what she was up to.

Taking the stairs two at a time, she hurried down the hall toward Carolina and Archer's room. She was almost to the door when she heard the raised voices.

"How did you get in here?" Carolina said, sounding surprised and angry, and Alexa realized with a start, fear. "I want to be left alone."

She heard something heavy hit the floor with a crash, muffling the other person's voice.

"Are you crazy? Don't come near me." There was panic in Carolina's voice. "Stay back!"

Alexa remembered what she'd seen in Carolina's future and grabbed the doorknob. Locked. She struggled to get her key from her pocket as she heard something else hit the floor then Carolina's scream. She fumbled the key into the lock and turned it. The lock clicked and as she started to turn the knob, she heard another bloodcurdling scream from Carolina and the horrible sound of glass shattering.

She shoved the door and it swung in as Carolina's scream ended in a thud beyond the gaping hole where the window had been.

The room was empty. Where had the person Carolina had been arguing with gone?

Alexa rushed to the window to stare down

into the darkness. She could make out a crumpled shape far below. She started to turn, to run downstairs to get help, even though she knew Carolina was beyond help.

But before she could move, she heard a panel slide open in the wall and was grabbed from behind, a wet cloth clamped down over her mouth and nose. No! The room began to dim and then the lights went out. As she slumped to the floor, her last thought was of Marshall.

Chapter Thirteen

Marshall sat out on his porch, drinking a cold beer, staring at the Wellington mansion with all its lights on, thinking about Alexa. Worrying about her.

He hated the way he'd left things. He told himself the worst he could do was go over there this late at night and tell her how he felt about her.

He reminded himself that she wasn't even speaking to him. Not to mention she had enough problems at the moment. Given what they'd learned about the Wellingtons, he wasn't sure that bad blood had been passed down. If so, then the latest Sierra Wellington could be more dangerous than even Alexa suspected.

Alexa needed him. Right. Even after being drugged and hit on the head and knocked out, it hadn't scared Alexa off.

Yep, all the woman needed was for him

to storm over there and tell her that he was in love with her. In love with a woman who lived in another state, who may or may not see dead people and who didn't have a clue how he felt and probably didn't feel the same way about him.

She'd made it pretty clear she didn't want to see him again.

The light was still on in Alexa's room.

He took another sip of his beer. Clearly she couldn't sleep any better than he could on this hot August night.

He waited, half hoping she'd have a nightmare and come running across the pasture. He ached to kiss her, to hold her in his arms, to make love to her again.

Well, he wasn't going over there, he told himself as he finished his beer and got to his feet. If she wanted to see him, she knew where he lived.

He stared at the lights on over at the mansion, then at his watch and swore. Like hell he wasn't going over there. She might kick him out, but first she was going to hear what he had to say. He loved her, by damn, and it was time he told her.

Slapping his Stetson on his head, he headed across the pasture. He hadn't gone far when he heard a terrifying scream, followed only a few minutes later by gunfire.

He'd reached the rocks and bushes that covered the secret entry to the basement when he saw Jayden come stumbling out the front door of the house, a gun in his hand. Ducking down, he opened the door and slipped inside. His only thought was finding Alexa.

THE STENCH WAS UNBEARABLE. Worse, Alexa woke to find not only that she was trapped in the tunnel cage, but also she wasn't alone.

She could feel something unearthly huddled in the dark, back corner, an old woman, her breathing ragged, her mental anguish palpable.

Alexa's captor had left a flashlight lying on the floor of the tunnel, its beam turned toward the opposite wall. There was just enough light to see where she was, but beyond that faint beam was nothing but pockets of darkness.

Don't turn around. Don't—

She screamed as she felt the woman grasp her ankle. Alexa tried frantically to pull away as the woman clawed at her, pulling herself to her feet and turning Alexa to face her.

Alexa squeezed her eyes shut, willing herself not to open them, not wanting to look into the tortured eyes of the first Sierra Wellington. A scream rose in her throat but died off as she heard the sound of footfalls coming down the tunnel. She didn't dare open her eyes, afraid that it was a trick of either the spirits in this house—or her own imagination.

"Alexa?"

Marshall. Her eyes flew open. She blinked. She was alone in the cage and Marshall had found a piece of pipe and was breaking the lock. Moments later she was in his arms.

"What the hell is going on over here?" he demanded. "I heard gunshots."

"Someone killed Carolina, then they grabbed me...." Gunshots? "We have to find my brother." The words were barely out before they both turned at the sound of someone coming toward them from the house side of the tunnel.

MARSHALL WISHED HE HAD more of a weapon than the piece of pipe he'd used to open the cage door. He grabbed a flashlight from the floor, the batteries low, the beam faint. He turned it off as he pulled Alexa behind him.

"It's just me," came a voice, then a flashlight blinked on a half-dozen yards down the tunnel.

"Devlin," Alexa said.

"Alexa?" Devlin asked as Marshall turned on the flashlight again and Devlin moved toward them. "Thank God it's you and not Sierra. What are you doing down here?"

"You don't know?" Alexa asked.

He shook his head, grimacing as he glanced toward the cage. "Someone put you in there? What is going on? All hell has broken loose upstairs. Did you know Carolina killed herself?"

"Or someone in this house killed her," Alexa said. "Have you seen my brother?"

"No." Devlin looked confused. "But Sierra is looking for you and she has a gun."

"My brother." She tried to push past Marshall to run toward the entrance to the house, but he held her back.

"Listen," he said. They all fell silent, he and Devlin turning off their flashlights as they heard someone come down into the tunnel. A light shone at the other end, illuminating Sierra. She had a flashlight in one hand, a gun in the other.

"Landon?" she called. "Alexa? Anyone down here?"

Marshall held Alexa against him. He could

feel her holding her breath, just as he was. Devlin must have been doing the same.

Sierra stood there for a long moment, then turned and retreated back up the stairs to the main floor. They waited until they heard the door close before any of them made a sound.

"We have to get out of here," Devlin said.

"No, I have to find my brother," Alexa argued.

"Sierra doesn't know where he is," Marshall assured her. "He must have gotten out of the house."

"Marshall's right," Devlin agreed. "You can't help him if you run into Sierra and she kills you. Come on. Once we get out of here, we can call for help." He pointed his flashlight toward the exit by the pond. "Get Alexa out. I'll be right behind you."

ALEXA CAUGHT MOVEMENT behind them. Devlin had pulled a gun, striking Marshall in the head. Marshall let out a groan of pain and fell at her feet.

"What are you doing?" she cried and dropped beside the cowboy.

Devlin jerked her to her feet, jabbing her with the barrel of the gun. "Unless you want me to shoot him, shut up and come with me."

She looked into his eyes in the light from Marshall's dropped flashlight and knew Devlin was more than capable of murder. "You're the one who locked me in that cage."

"I'm going to do worse if you don't come with me now."

She touched Marshall's cheek. He was still breathing. Then she rose and let Devlin drag her out of the tunnel.

She feared her brother might still be in the house, maybe even looking for her, or that Devlin had already taken care of him. And where were the others? But she didn't argue as they climbed up out of the tunnel and into the faint moonlight.

Breathing in the fresh air, filling her lungs, she tried to dispel her fear as well as the smell and memory of the cage and the old woman in there.

She looked toward the house and saw that all the lights were on. Someone was beside the house and she could hear what sounded like heart-wrenching sobs. Archer. He was kneeling on the ground under the window where Carolina had fallen. He was holding her body, rocking and wailing.

The sound sent a sliver of ice down her spine.

Devlin was standing in the moonlight, a gun in his hand, a strange look on his face.

"You're working with Sierra?" Alexa asked in confusion.

Devlin scoffed. "Sierra is a *Wellington*." There was contempt in his tone. "Her father destroyed mine."

"Yours?" His name hadn't been on the list of those people who'd been bilked by J. A. Wellington. "I don't understand. I thought your father owned a vineyard."

"That's my stepfather. He adopted me after he bought my father's vineyard for pennies on the dollar—and got my mother in the deal as well. My father is a drunk who spends most of his time in prison, and all because J. A. Wellington swindled him just like he did Carolina's father."

"You and Carolina?" Alexa said.

Devlin smiled. "It was so easy to get close to Sierra. She didn't have any idea who we were."

"So this is all about the money," Alexa said.

"That and justice. I was more into the money. Carolina…" He shrugged.

Alexa saw it now and let out a small gasp. "You killed her."

"Sierra said you were psychic, that you

knew things." Devlin frowned and took a step back, the gun in his hand not quite as steady. "I told Carolina we had to get rid of you right away. But she talked me into waiting. She wanted to know her future." He suddenly looked alarmed. "You saw that she was going to die, didn't you? That's why she was freaking."

"You killed her because you wanted the money all to yourself?" Alexa asked.

"You know that's not why. This is all your fault," Devlin said, anger making his perfect features look inhuman. "You made her think the money was cursed and that if either of us took it…" He shook his head. "She wanted to burn the place down, the money with it."

"But you had already found the money. No," she said as she realized why Devlin had abducted her. "*Carolina* found the money. She moved it and then wouldn't tell you where. You think I can tell you where she hid it."

He looked surprised and nervous. "You're good."

"And Sierra?" Alexa asked. "She was looking for the money too."

Devlin snorted. "I thought her old man had told her where it was, but I guess not." He raised the gun until the barrel was pointed at her face. "But now you are going to tell me where it's hidden."

"Why don't I tell you your future instead," Alexa said, stalling. She had no idea where the money was hidden. It hadn't taken any psychic talent to see through Devlin.

"I know my future," he said with a quick shake of his head. "I'm going to be filthy rich. I'm never going to have to ask my stepfather for another dime."

"You're not going to kill me because then you will never know where the money is hidden."

For a moment Devlin looked uncertain, but then he smiled. "You're right. I'm not going to kill you. I'm going to go back in and kill your boyfriend and then your brother. Yes, I know where he is. I left him bound and gagged in another part of the basement."

Alexa felt only a moment's relief.

"So what's it going to be?" he demanded.

"Take him to the money." With a start, Alexa saw her mother materialize behind him.

"What?" Devlin demanded. "Are you trying to freak me out or something?"

She knew she had gone pale. She tried to

still her trembling as she stared at the apparition of her mother behind him.

"Tell him where the money is," her mother said, and yet the sound didn't come from her lips but seemed to come from inside Alexa's own head.

She closed her eyes, shaking her head, not wanting to hear her mother's voice, not wanting to see her mother. Only crazy people saw the dead, talked to the dead.

"Crazy people and some clairvoyants," her mother said. "Tell him you will take him to the money."

Alexa hadn't realized that she'd spoken.

"Who are you talking to?" Devlin demanded, looking worried.

"My mother."

"I thought your mother was—" He glanced over his shoulder. "If you think you can scare me—"

"She told me to take you to the money."

He glanced around, nervous and unsure. "She knows where it is?"

"She said she will lead me to it."

Alexa could tell he desperately wanted to believe what she was saying was true. But like a lot of people, he didn't believe in ghosts. Or at least he didn't want to.

"This had better not be a trick," he warned.

"Lead him down to the pond," her mother said.

They hadn't gone but a few steps when Alexa saw Marshall moving through the darkness of the cottonwoods. He had the piece of pipe. Marshall had the piece of pipe he'd used to free her. She was never so happy to see anyone in her life.

Marshall came out of the trees quickly, moving with a swiftness and sureness of a man on a mission.

Devlin never knew what hit him.

Marshall dragged her into his arms. "Alexa, I love you. I don't care that this is probably the worse possible time to tell you how I feel but—"

Suddenly they were surrounded by agents of the U.S. Department of the Treasury.

Epilogue

The rest of the night was a blur. It wasn't until the next morning, sitting in Marshall's warm kitchen having a cup of coffee that Alexa finally felt it was over.

Last night, after the federal agents had released them, Marshall had brought her back here. They'd made love in his bed upstairs. She'd told him she loved him.

"I still can't believe Jayden is with the Department of the Treasury," Marshall said as he took a chair across from her. Jayden had been wounded by Devlin, but was going to live. Devlin had been taken into custody.

"Last night when I saw Sierra with that gun… I guess we all thought the worst of her when she was only trying to find Landon and save him from Devlin."

Marshall nodded. "So Jayden and Sierra weren't having an affair?"

"Apparently not," she said and took a sip of

her coffee. Sunlight streamed in the windows, warming her more than the coffee. "Sierra was working with the feds by coming back to the house and pretending to open a bed-and-breakfast."

"And Landon didn't know?"

Alexa shook her head. "Sierra said she wasn't allowed to tell him anything. Apparently when Devlin and Carolina befriended her, the feds had already been watching the whole bunch of them. It had been easy to let Devlin and Carolina think it was their idea to come to Montana to help renovate the house for a bed-and-breakfast."

"So all the spouses were in the dark?"

"I guess so, though I suspect at least Archer must have known what was going on," she said. "I think that's what he and Carolina argued about that night before Devlin killed her and got out of the room through one of the secret passages only to come back for me."

"How is Landon taking all this?"

"I don't know. I only got to see him for a few minutes after the agents brought him up out of the basement, where Devlin had left him. I think he is probably in as much shock as the rest of us."

Marshall reached across the table and took her hand. "A lot happened last night."

She met his gaze, recalling with a start that he'd seen her mother standing behind her that day he rode by on his horse. "You saw her last night, didn't you?"

He nodded. "Only this time, I knew that feeling of evil I'd felt wasn't coming from her."

"No," Alexa agreed. She had faced her greatest fear in that house—seeing her mother again. She'd also quit denying that she hadn't inherited her mother's gift. "She helped save us last night."

Marshall nodded. "By leading you and Devlin down to the pond, I was able to follow in the trees."

Alexa looked into this man's bottomless dark eyes and felt more peace than she had ever known. He knew all her secrets and yet he was still here. He'd saved her life last night and he'd told her that he loved her. But where did they go from here? Or did they?

At a knock at the door, she heard her brother call out her name.

Landon looked the worse for wear this morning. Like her, she doubted he'd had much sleep. He came in and took the coffee

Marshall offered him then Marshall left the two of them to talk in the living room.

"Are you all right?" Alexa asked her brother. He seemed older somehow, not the young man she'd always felt she needed to protect.

"I've been better."

"And Sierra?"

He shook his head.

"I still can't believe Devlin set the place on fire," Alexa said. She could still smell the smoke in the air. She'd avoided looking at what remained of Wellington Manor and so had Marshall. Neither of them had been sorry to see the place burn.

"That's Sierra's story anyway," Landon said.

"You can't think she set the fire? I thought she really cared about the house and the things in it," Alexa said, remembering the scene with the wine glass she'd broken.

"Who knows what Sierra cared about and how much was all an act?" Landon said. "I can forgive her for not telling me what was really going on. But there are other things…. I didn't want to admit that I rushed into the marriage. Now I realize that Sierra needed a husband in order to come back to Wellington Manor."

"But wasn't that the feds pushing her to make those hasty decisions?"

Landon laughed softly. "Let's be honest. Sierra married me for my inheritance just in case she couldn't find her father's money he stole. As for Jayden, sure she was meeting with him some of those nights, but a lot of them she was looking for that money, hoping she found it first. I think we both know what she would have done with it."

"Have the agents found the money yet?"

"Carolina had called them and told them she'd buried it by the pond. Jayden didn't get the word until Carolina had already been killed. When he moved in to arrest Devlin, that's when he was shot and Sierra took his gun, fearing Devlin would be coming after her next."

"When I saw her in the basement, she was looking for you and me."

He smiled. "She was responsible for my accidents. I'm just lucky she didn't kill me, that way she could have at least had my money, and possibly her father's as well."

"I'm sorry."

"I've already told Sierra that I'm filing for

a divorce. You'll be happy that I'm going back to college. The one thing I am certain of is that the woman I fell in love with doesn't exist. I'm just sorry I put you in such a terrible position. I could have gotten you killed and all because I was so sure—"

"You were right. I am like Mother."

He stared at her in surprise.

"I have no control over it, still am afraid of it and not sure I want to use it, but I'm no longer denying its presence. I'm sorry I lied to you."

"Mother would be so happy if she knew."

"She knows."

"And Marshall?" her brother asked.

She nodded and smiled. "I'm in love with him. I'm not sure where it's going…."

"I'm happy for you, sis."

THE MOMENT EMMA SAW THE sheriff's expression she knew. "Come in," she said, stepping back and letting McCall enter.

"The woman Aggie believed was Laura Chisholm got away, didn't she?" Emma asked as she led the sheriff into the kitchen, where Hoyt was sitting at the table, having a cup of coffee and some homemade blueberry crumble cake.

"She was gone when the police got there," McCall said after declining both coffee and coffee cake. "She'd cleaned out the place so she must have found out that Aggie was making inquiries about her."

Emma sighed. "So it wouldn't have made any difference even if Aggie and I had gone to Billings."

Hoyt sent her a look that said he would never have let her go anywhere. He'd become suspicious after overhearing Emma on the phone and had called the sheriff, suspecting what Emma was up to. The man knew her too well.

Maybe if she hadn't said she was going to bake his favorite cookies…

Well, it was too late to start second-guessing her mistakes.

"What about Aggie?" she asked the sheriff.

"We're still dragging the river for her body."

No luck. That didn't surprise Emma. She would bet that Aggie Wells might have more in common with Laura Chisholm than anyone knew. Laura had said she was afraid of water. Emma suspected Aggie swam like a fish—even injured.

"If Aggie contacts you again—" the sheriff began.

"I'm to call you at once," Emma said, cutting her off.

"Yep, but that was what you were supposed to do this last time," Hoyt said.

The sheriff and Hoyt both looked at her as if they knew Emma would do whatever she decided to do and to hell with the consequences.

"I'll try to keep better track of her," Hoyt told the sheriff.

"For how long?" Emma demanded. "You have a ranch to run and now both Aggie and some woman who may or may not be your first, jealous, murderous wife, back from the grave, are out there. With one, if not both of them, wanting me dead."

"The boys can run the ranch just fine without me," Hoyt said.

"Well, I can tell you right now, I won't have you watching over me like I'm one of your horses. I won't be corralled." With that Emma stormed out of the room, only to have Hoyt follow her up to their bedroom and take her in his arms.

"You have to forgive me," Hoyt said as he pulled her close.

"Forgive you for what?" Emma asked, all her earlier anger evaporating the moment he held her.

"You blame me for what happened to Aggie. But Emma, if you had come to me and told me you were going to meet her—"

"You would have stopped me."

He fell silent. "You're my wife. I want to protect you."

"You Chisholm men. You all love a woman in trouble. But Hoyt Chisholm, you fell in love with a strong, independent woman—just like four of your sons have done."

"I know. What do you want me to do, Emma? I can't take the chance that there is someone out there who wants you dead and that if I'm not around..."

"Yes?"

He sighed. "I know you can take care of yourself. That is one of the many things I love about you. But we're talking about a killer, Emma."

"A killer who might never strike again."

"Or one who might strike tomorrow."

"Then I'll be ready tomorrow," Emma said. "And if I need you, I'll holler. It's time for you to be the rancher I married. I love nothing more than seeing you on a horse, doing what you love."

He smiled at her. "I've never met a woman like you."

"I know."

AFTER LANDON LEFT, MARSHALL came down to find Alexa standing at the window, staring out across the pasture at the smoldering remains of Wellington Manor. He was glad that soon, when he looked out this window, he would no longer see anything but the Montana horizon.

"Are you all right?" he asked as he put his arms around her to pull her close. He breathed in her freshly showered scent and told himself he couldn't bear the thought that she might go back to Spokane and he'd never see her again.

"I'm fine. Landon's divorcing Sierra but he seems stronger now. I'm not worried about him anymore. I guess it's finally over."

"That's funny because I was just thinking that some things were just beginning," he said as he turned her in his arms to look into her beautiful face. "I guess I should ask you, though, since I forget that you can see the future."

She smiled at him. "Not if I'm too close to it. Like I am with you."

"So then you don't know what's going to happen now?"

She laughed. "You're going to kiss me?"

He looked into her violet eyes and saw desire and love burning brightly. He could see the two of them living in this house, raising children who would one day ride across this land, their land, with the two of them, their lives blessed through all the love he and Alexa had to share.

"Or did you have something else in mind?" she asked.

He laughed. "Apparently I'm able to see the future better than you can."

"Oh?"

He nodded. "Want me to tell you about it?"

She shook her head. "No, I want you to surprise me."

And he did.

* * * * *

LARGER-PRINT BOOKS!
GET 2 FREE LARGER-PRINT NOVELS PLUS
2 FREE GIFTS!

◆ Harlequin®

INTRIGUE®

BREATHTAKING ROMANTIC SUSPENSE

HILPI1B